Where the Heart Is

Where the Heart Is

JO KNOWLES

CANDLEWICK PRESS

Copyright © 2019 by Jo Knowles

First paperback edition 2021

Library of Congress Catalog Card Number 2018961168
ISBN 978-1-5362-0003-4 (hardcover)
ISBN 978-1-5362-1902-9 (paperback)

21 22 23 24 25 26 TRC 10 9 8 7 6 5 4 3 2 1

Printed in Eagan, MN, USA

This book was typeset in Dante MT.

Candlewick Press
99 Dover Street
Somerville, Massachusetts 02144

www.candlewick.com

For Stephanie,
best sister, best friend.
Thank you for the bike — and so much more.
I love you.
xoxo

⸂ Chapter One ⸃

I was six years old when I got engaged to Micah Sasaki. It was during coffee hour at church, when the adults were busy in the fellowship hall, eating banana bread and gossiping and letting the kids run wild on the front lawn. We were playing Sardines. I found Micah under the lilac bushes by the steps and we huddled together, waiting to be found. We held hands and giggled quietly each time we heard footsteps and heavy breathing as someone ran past.

We waited like that for a long time, and then, out of the blue, Micah whispered, "I love you, Rachel." His breath smelled like bananas.

He squeezed my hand, and my small heart thumped in my chest as if it were a hummingbird trapped inside.

"Do you want to marry me?" he asked.

"Yes!" I said without hesitation.

He was my first and best friend, and my favorite neighbor. We liked almost all the same games and even the same food. Marriage made perfect sense.

"Move over!" Nadia Collins said, interrupting our engagement.

Micah and I smiled at each other and squished even closer together. The lilac bushes were in full bloom, and the smell of the blossoms engulfed us each time someone jostled the branches.

Cole Jenkins found us next. Then a few others, and then the game was over. We all climbed out from under the bushes, but before we went back inside, Micah gave me a lilac and kissed me on the cheek. Then we found our parents and told them the news.

They laughed and said, "How sweet," as if it were a silly joke.

Micah got mad and stomped off, which only made the grown-ups laugh harder.

I found Micah back under the lilac bushes, red-faced. "They don't know anything," I told him.

"We'll always be together," he said. "Right?"

I climbed under the branches and sat next to him and held his hand again. "Always," I said. We sat like that until our parents came and found us and apologized for being insensitive.

Even though that was six years ago, sometimes one of our parents will bring it up, asking us in a jokey kind of way how the wedding plans are going. Micah always blushes and smiles awkwardly, and maybe even a little hopefully. But more and more, I'm filled with guilt. Because deep down, as much as I love Micah, I know it will never happen.

"Rachel, wake up right now!" my sister yells, pounding on my door.

I sit up and feel dizzy. A familiar panic rises in my chest. I can't believe I'm going to be late for school *again*.

Then I remember. Today is the first day of summer! Not only that: it's my thirteenth birthday.

Ivy bangs on my door again.

"There's no school!" I yell back. "Remember? Summer!"

"Mom wants us up for something else!" she calls. "So get up!"

I bet she made me birthday pancakes. I sniff and smell something delicious. Maybe waffles.

Outside my window, the leaves are bright green and the birds chirp extra loudly. It's like the whole outside woke up for summer vacation. Better yet, for my birthday. Warm, sunny days stretch out before me. No more getting up early to catch the bus. No more homework. No more math class with Mr. Drake, who hates me because I never show my work and he thinks I cheat because I still get the right answers. No more worries! Plus I'm a teenager now. I can get more babysitting jobs. I can save money for a better bike than the crappy one my dad scavenged from the dump when I was eight. I can—

"Rachel, would you *get up?*" Ivy yells through my door again. "The new neighbors are here!"

I peer through my window. Across the street, a moving truck pulls into the long driveway where construction has been going on all year. The house was built on a long, sloping hill in the field we've used for sledding every winter and riding my old pony Rainbow in the summer. It was designed to look like a rustic barn, but we peeked through the windows after the workers went home one night and there is nothing rustic about it inside. There are fancy marble counters in the kitchen, and the bathrooms are like the ones you only see on TV, with glass bowls for sinks instead of regular old white porcelain ones. The floors are so polished, they showed the reflection of the windows, as well as our heads, when we peeked through the glass.

"Wow," I remember Micah saying the first time we looked in.

"They must be loaded," Ivy said.

"Why on earth would they move here?" I asked.

They were a mystery, and the whole neighborhood was speculating about who these people could be and where they might come from. Behind the house, they'd built a real barn, with stables, several little sheds, and what looked like a chicken coop. They seemed to be planning on having lots of animals, which Ivy was very excited about. Micah and I made up a whole story about the types of animals they'd have. We decided the new neighbors were rare animal collectors and they'd have tigers and zebras and things, but that got Ivy all upset, so we stopped.

The cat meows from the foot of my bed when I get up and step into my slippers. George hates being woken up as much as I do.

"I'm coming!" I yell.

I pull my hair into a ponytail. "Go back to sleep," I tell George. "It's summer!"

He walks in a circle and settles down again in his

little nest in the squares of sunlight coming through my window.

Downstairs, the sweet smell from the kitchen is even stronger.

"Go back up and get dressed, Rachel," my mom says, pushing me away before I can go into the kitchen to see what she's made. She has on a red apron that's covered in flour. There's some on her face, too.

"We need to take a pie over to welcome the new neighbors, and it's almost finished. I want you dressed so we can all go over together to introduce ourselves."

Pie? So that's what was baking. Not my birthday breakfast? I hope she didn't make an extra pie for my birthday cake. Pie is good, but not for birthdays. I want a tall layered cake with thick frosting and fourteen candles because you always have to have one to grow on. Licking syrupy fruit off a candle just isn't the same as licking off frosting.

I wait a minute before going back upstairs. I look around for the familiar birthday banner my mom made, which she hangs from the ceiling on the morning of our birthdays. It isn't in the usual place above the kitchen table. Maybe because this is a special year, we'll eat in the dining room, which we only use to celebrate big holidays. The rest of the time, the dining-room table is piled with mail and newspapers and bills and home-work and lots of other junk.

"Go on!" my mom says, still not wishing me a happy birthday.

I turn away from her slowly and take my time walking back to the stairs, just to give her a chance to remember.

"Hustle your buns!" she yells at me.

Sheesh.

From my bedroom window, I watch the new owners boss the movers around. They don't seem very promising. They look too old to have kids our age, which is fine with me because I don't really feel like having to make new friends with someone who lives in a house like that. Just walking around, peeking in the windows and being that close to something so nice made me feel crappy about my holey sneakers and cutoff shorts. Micah said maybe they'd have older kids and I'd get their hand-me-downs. Whoop-de-do! It's bad enough I have to wear the things family friends hand down to us, or cheap clothes my mom finds at the local thrift store. I get itchy just thinking about it. Micah says I sound like a snob when I complain. I tell him I'm just a clean freak, and he says that's what washing machines are for, which is a good point. But still. I'll never like wearing other people's old clothes. They have all these memories in them that I don't know about. Sometimes I wonder what interesting places they've been to. But mostly I try not to think about it.

"Rachel and Ivy, get down here!" my mom yells up the stairs.

I pull on my old shorts and a T-shirt and go to the bathroom to brush my teeth, but Ivy is already inside. I bang on the door, even though that'll probably make her stay in extra long.

"Mom's calling us!" I urge through the door. "Get moving!"

She finally opens the door and shines her clean teeth at me. "All yours, sucker!" she says.

I step in and get accosted by the smell of her poop. "You are so gross!" I scream. I hold my breath, grab my toothbrush, and run downstairs to use the other bathroom.

"Can we *please* get going?" my mom says when I finish brushing my teeth.

I glare at Ivy again. "So gross," I say again. "You're eight years old, not five."

"Everyone poops," she says. "Even eight-year-olds."

"Don't be disgusting," my mom says. "Now, let's go."

We follow her outside and down the driveway. Even from across the street, we can hear the new neighbors still giving orders to the movers, who roll furniture out of a massive moving truck. We weave through the parked trucks up the newly paved driveway. It smells like burning tar in the hot morning sun. Everything over here smells new.

"Hello?" my mom calls, stepping toward the neighbors.

The wife turns around. She looks like she's in her sixties or so. She's so tan that the creases in the wrinkles in her face look like someone made them with a dark-brown pen. Like she's spent so much time in the sun, her skin has turned to leather.

"We're your new neighbors from across the street," my mom says to the lady. "These are my kids, Rachel and Ivy. I'm Lydia Gartner."

The lady smiles, and her face lines deepen and darken even more. "Well, hello!" she says, all friendly. "It's so nice to meet you!"

"We baked you a pie," my mom says, holding it out. "Peaches aren't quite in season yet, so I hope you like strawberry rhubarb."

"So thoughtful of you." The lady takes the pie and smells it. "My name's Greer. Greer Townsend. My husband over there is Bev. Bev, honey, come meet our new neighbors!"

Bev seems like a strange name for a man. I wonder what it's short for. He has the same kind of tanned and wrinkly leather face as Greer. He's wearing bright-green shorts that have little white boats embroidered on them, and a matching white polo shirt. He looks like a guy you might see playing golf on TV. Greer has on a similar outfit, only a skirt, not shorts. It's pink, and I think it's a tennis skirt, the kind with shorts underneath.

Greer and Bev seem old but sporty. Just like the rest of their stuff, their clothes look brand-new. Like they haven't even been washed yet, or sweated in.

"How do you do?" Bev asks, reaching for my mother's hand.

I didn't know people said *How do you do?* in real life. He has a funny accent, like his voice is still being haunted by his rich English ancestors or something. Later I'll learn that he says things like *baaaaath* instead of *bath* and *lauuuuugh* instead of *laugh,* the way a sheep might if a sheep could talk.

Ivy holds out her hand and Bev shakes it, then mine. He squeezes pretty hard for an old man. His hand is soft and smooth, not like my parents' hands, which are rough from gardening and stacking wood and all the other outdoor work we all do.

"You have nice weather for moving day," my mom says. "Is there anything we can help you with?"

Greer nods distractedly and motions for a mover to be careful with a tiny wooden bookcase. "No, no, that's what the movers are for, dear," Greer says. "But thank you."

"Well, we'll leave you to it. Welcome to the neighborhood." My mom is acting so awkward, like she doesn't know how to behave around rich people.

"Thank you for the pie," Bev says, turning to walk up the driveway.

"We'll have to have you over for drinks when we're settled in," Greer adds.

"That would be lovely." My mom motions for us to go.

"Snobs," I say when we cross the road to our side.

"Don't say that," my mom says. "Just because people are wealthy doesn't make them snobs."

"They took away our sledding hill," I say.

"Oh, Rachel, it was never *ours*. We were lucky to be able to use it as long as we did."

Ivy runs ahead, but my mom and I walk slowly

up the driveway, with the weeds growing through the cracked pavement. Our old farmhouse is red, and the paint is peeling. Some of the shutters hang a little off-kilter. Even though we don't really live on a farm, my grandfather made a sign for the house, just like real farms have. My mom decided on the name Bittersweet Farm when she and my dad moved in, before Ivy and I were born. She had taken a walk on the property with my father and discovered bittersweet running all along the stone wall that ran next to the road and defined the property line years ago when it was still a working farm and the stone wall kept the cows and sheep from getting out. Every fall she cuts branches and makes bittersweet wreaths to hang on the walls throughout the house. The vines are full of bright-yellow shells that open up when they dry to reveal a red berry inside. My mom says they make our drafty old house feel cheerful on cold, dark days.

Whenever we come home from someplace, the sign welcomes us and reminds us that life isn't perfect, just like my mom always says. It's a little bitter and a little sweet.

We stop midway up the driveway to look at the sign, which also needs painting. My mom puts her hand on my shoulder. "Happy first day of summer," she says, squeezing.

But not *Happy birthday*.

In fact, the whole day no one says a word about me turning thirteen, and I finally realize that they've forgotten. Micah always says there's no such thing as lucky or unlucky numbers, but thirteen sure feels pretty unlucky so far.

❧ Chapter Two ❧

I always thought my tenth birthday would be remembered as the most awkward and disappointing in history, but my thirteenth takes the cake. At least when I turned ten, everyone remembered. But it was really the best day for my mom, not me. She called me downstairs for my "birthday meal," but instead of having anything ready, she was holding a winter scarf.

"Close your eyes and let me cover your face," she said, wrapping the scarf around my head.

It was an old woolen scarf she'd knitted for my dad years ago when they were still dating. It was brown with white stripes and smelled like an ancient sheep. It scratched my cheeks.

"Now let me lead you outside," my mom said.

"What's happening?" Ivy asked as she bounded into the room. "Why are you tying up Rachel?"

"I'm not tying her up. I'm covering her eyes so she can't see."

"How come?"

"We have a special birthday present for her."

"Is it outside?"

"Yes."

The door slammed, and I heard Ivy *woot* in the distance.

I hoped that meant I was getting a new bike.

My mom led me slowly across the room and out the front door, down the old loose and wobbly stone steps.

"Just let me lead you," my mom said, guiding me down the driveway.

"Are you ready?" she called out to someone in the distance.

"Ready when you are!" my dad replied.

My mom stopped me and put her hands on my shoulders. The scarf was really starting to itch now, and the smell was making me feel funny.

"Here we go," she said, untying the scarf.

I blinked a few times and looked around. We were at the foot of the driveway. At one corner was a horse trailer and next to it was my dad, standing with a tiny horse. It was black and white and had a bright-green halter.

"What's that?" I asked.

The tiny horse stared at me suspiciously.

My dad was clutching the halter tightly, as if he knew the horse might bolt at any second.

"It's your birthday present!" my mom said. Tears slipped down the side of her face. "Your very own pony. His name is Rainbow. Isn't he just beautiful?"

He blinked at me as I stepped closer. *Beautiful* wasn't the word I would have picked. He was cute, though. He nodded his head at me and I patted his nose. The hairs around his eyes were gray, and I wondered how old he was. Surely not a "new" pony like you might expect a kid might get for her birthday.

"He's a rescue," my mom said. "He's going to need a lot of love and patience." She hugged him then, and I could tell without a doubt that this was definitely a present for her and not me.

The favorite story my mom likes to tell about her childhood is the day she got her own pony, Buddy. The story goes that for three whole years she prayed every night for a horse. Finally, on her tenth birthday, her prayers were answered. My grandfather took her out to the front lawn on the morning of her birthday, a scarf wrapped over her eyes, and when he took it off, there was Buddy, a palomino pony with a big brown patch over one side of his face and all white on the other. There's an old photo of my mom on the back of Buddy that she keeps on the mantel in the living room. She's sitting backward and leaning forward, resting an open book on his rump. He's tethered to a stake in the ground, eating grass on the front lawn of the house she grew up in. This is the way I picture my mom's entire childhood: carefree summers sitting on Buddy, reading the days away. The problem is, it's how she's always envisioned mine, too.

Rainbow sniffed my hand, then licked it, leaving a trail of sticky saliva.

My mom pulled a plastic bag filled with baby carrots out of her pocket and handed them to me. "Put one in the palm of your hand and hold it out flat so he doesn't nip you," she said. "Like this."

I put a carrot in my hand and held it out, and Rainbow slurped it up with his big velvety lips.

"I want to try!" Ivy yelled. Rainbow reared his head at the sound and stepped back, frightened.

"Don't scare him, Ivy. You have to use a gentle voice," my mom said.

"Hi, Rainbow," Ivy whispered, letting him take a carrot from her hand.

We spent the rest of the day preparing a stall for him in the old barn behind the house, and Ivy and I took turns walking him on his lead while the other rode bareback. My mom said we needed to spend a lot of gentle, loving time with him in order to bond. But I think Rainbow would be friends with anyone with a carrot and a soft voice. My favorite thing to do with him was put Ivy on his back and tie him to a stake in the grass, just like in my mom's photo. Then I'd sit in my mom's old plastic lawn chair and read to Ivy while she braided the bits of mane she could reach.

For my eleventh birthday, I got a new bridle for Rainbow, since the one he came with was so worn, the leather reins kept splitting in two and my mom kept having to patch them together with duct tape. I don't even know why I bothered to try to ride him, he was so fat and lazy. The girth on the old saddle he came with barely stretched over his round belly. No one knew how old he really was, but the guess was that he was in his twenties. There was something special about him, though, and whenever I came toward him with his bridle, he'd sniff my hand for a treat and sometimes lick it fondly, like he did the first time we met. I knew it was his way of accepting me, even though I was sure he preferred being read to in the grass than taking me for rides. I was allowed to ride him to the bottom of the field across the street, but it was agony getting him to go. The only time he picked up speed was when we turned around and he knew he was heading for home. Then he would trot slowly with his ears perked up and pointed straight for the barn, where he knew my mom was waiting with a sugar cube. Riding in the field felt like our special time, and sometimes I'd sing "Over the Rainbow" to him as we trudged along. I know it sounds silly, but I think it made him feel special.

For my twelfth birthday, I got a new saddle pad for Rainbow, which was white and was supposed to look like sheep's wool but was fake. It made his old saddle look even more shabby. But by then it didn't matter because Rainbow had decided he was done with giving me rides and refused to cross the street to the field, even when I swatted him lightly with a crop my mom made out of a stick. Not even the promise of sugar cubes and singing his favorite song would work.

"He's an old guy," my mom said to me when I finally gave up trying. "But you got a lot of rides out of him. Maybe you should just sit on him and read, like I did on Buddy."

"OK," I said. But instead I put Ivy on his back and read out loud because I didn't like to read alone the way my mom did. It was more fun sharing stories than reading them by myself.

But today, on my thirteenth birthday, all I get is a phone call from Micah, who sings "Happy Birthday" in an operatic voice so loud I have to hold the phone away from my ear.

"Thanks for remembering," I say.

"What'd you get?" he asks.

I don't want to answer at first. But Micah is patient. Silence never makes him uncomfortable like it does me.

"Nothing," I finally say. "I guess they all forgot."

"Your parents? That's impossible. I bet your mom is just waiting for some special moment to surprise you. She always does stuff like that. Remember the scavenger hunt when you turned eleven? You were convinced you weren't getting a present, but your mom hid all those notes that led to Rainbow's new bridle. That was the best! I bet they have something like that planned."

"Maybe." But it's already seven thirty and we had dinner and it just seems like if there was going to be a surprise, it would have happened by now.

"Well, I love you," Micah says. "And you should have invited me over because I could have brought you your present and then your family would have clued in and felt guilty and probably gone out and bought you a huge cake or something."

"It's OK—they can't afford it anyway. I would have at least liked a homemade card, though."

"Sorry, Rachel. That stinks."

We get off the phone, and I go over to my window to breathe some cool air. It's dusk, but across the street I can see a big horse trailer in our neighbors' driveway. The new barn they built has three stalls with actual wood floors, not dirt like the ones in our old barn. I bet it's a lot easier to muck out the stalls when you have a wood floor.

As I look out the window, feeling sorry for myself, the sky gets darker and darker. And then a strange, flickering light comes from the bottom of the driveway. Then another. Three altogether, marching toward my window. They're sparklers. As they get closer, I can see my mom, dad, and Ivy each carrying one, swirling them in the air to make circles and hearts that last just a second before dimming into black. Then my dad spells out *Rachel* before his sizzles out and he has to light another.

"Happy birthday to you," they begin to sing as they

approach my window. *"Happy birthday to you. Happy birthday, dear Rachel. Happy birthday to you."*

"Come on out and see what we got you," my mom calls.

"Did you think we forgot?" Ivy says. "You didn't, did you?"

"Of course not!" I lie happily.

I quickly text Micah, *They remembered!* and run outside.

"Stay here while I go get your present," Ivy says, all excited. "Sorry to keep you waiting, but I wanted it to be dark. You have to guess the surprise before you can see it."

"I hope you didn't think we forgot," my mom says.

I shrug. "Maybe. But I'm glad you didn't."

"Ivy's been planning this for days," my dad says. "Even the sparklers were her idea."

My mom and dad stand on either side of me, squeezing me tight. It's a good sandwich to be in, feeling love from both sides like that, when no one can see us so I don't have to be embarrassed.

"Are you excited?" my dad asks.

"I can't really imagine what it could be," I say.

"Your sister put a lot of work into it, so if you don't love it, pretend to anyway," my mom says.

I wish she didn't feel like she had to tell me that.

Pretty soon there's a familiar *click click click*ing sound a bike makes when you're coasting along, and then I can see reflectors shining as Ivy begins pedaling toward me, then a light flicks on the front. She squeaks the brakes just before she gently bumps the front tire into me.

"Ta-da!" Ivy steps off and flails her arms like a game show host presenting a prize.

My dad runs into the house and turns the outside lights on so we can see better.

"I saw an ad in the *PennySaver* and grabbed it quick before anyone else could," my dad says. "Ivy has been making all the repairs, greasing the chain and making it as good as new."

"Wow," I say. "Thanks!"

"Try it out!" Ivy says. "It's a million times better than your old piece of junk."

"Ivy!" my mom says.

"Well, it is!"

My old bike really is a piece of junk. Riding to Micah's is a huge risk because I never know if the chain will fall off or the worn brakes will give out when I go down the big hill on the way to his house and I'll end up in a ditch. Plus it's way too small for me, so my knees rise up high when I pedal and I look ridiculous.

I climb on, and the seat is already set just right for me. Ivy looks genuinely excited. Usually when she smiles, it means she has set up some sort of prank, but on holidays like Christmas and my birthday, I can usually rely on her smile being genuine.

"Do you like the light on the handlebar? That's my favorite. It's why we had to wait until tonight to give it to you!" Ivy points to a flashlight she duct-taped to the handlebars.

I click the light off and on. "Yeah!" I ride in a circle around the driveway, the flashlight casting a yellow glow in the space a few feet in front of me, as they all watch.

"What do you think?" Ivy asks.

"It's great!" I say. "I love it!"

After I ride around for a bit, my dad leads us out to the back porch, where my mom has hung my birthday banner after all. There's a cake with lots of frosting, and a vase with wildflowers set in the middle of the table surrounded by homemade cards with funny drawings. There's even a card from old Rainbow.

My thirteenth birthday is pretty good after all. Maybe the best one yet. I can't wait to ride my bike to Micah's and show it off.

That night, after I help clean up, I go to my room and lie in bed. A warm breeze drifts through my window. My parents' bedroom is below mine and I can hear their bedtime voices from their open window, but not enough to make out what they're saying. The sound steadily gets louder and eventually turns into one of their fights. A door slams, and footsteps pound through the house.

Ivy peeks her head through my bedroom door. "Did you hear that?" she asks.

"The sound, not the words," I say.

"They're fighting about money again."

"What else is new?" I ask.

"I hate it," she says.

"They're just stressed—don't worry. They still love each other."

"They sure don't sound like it," she says. "They sound like they hate each other."

"We fight all the time, and we don't hate each other."

"That's different."

"How?"

"Sisters are supposed to fight and stuff. Not Mom and Dad."

"It'll be OK," I say. "Try not to worry."

"Aren't you worried?"

"I'll worry for you, OK? Now go to bed."

She hangs her head sadly. "All right. G'night," she says, and sulks off down the hall.

"Thanks again for the bike!" I call after her. But I don't hear a reply.

The house is quiet again, but I can't sleep. I wait and wait until finally I hear the floorboards creak below and my parents' voices again. They get low and quiet, and I can tell they're making up. I hope Ivy is still awake so she can hear, too.

↫ Chapter Three ↬

"This is pretty great!" Micah says when I ride my bike to his house the next day.

Micah always gets new stuff when he outgrows something. He never has to sort through hand-me-down bags like I do. He probably doesn't even know what one is.

"Let's go for a ride," he says. "To celebrate summer. We can pack a picnic."

I follow him inside. His parents aren't home, so we raid the kitchen for snacks. We make peanut butter, lettuce, and mayonnaise sandwiches. They're my mom's favorite and have become mine, too. The first time I made one for Micah, he almost threw up when I told him what it was. But then he took another bite and realized how delicious they are. We add a bag of chips and half a box of ginger cookies. Then we put it all in Micah's backpack and head out.

I follow behind Micah and get used to my bike, trying the gears and testing the brakes just to make sure they really work. I'm so used to being scared on my old bike that I can't seem to stop worrying.

We didn't agree on where to go, but I have a hunch we'll end up at our usual place, the small local beach that's only a short ride away.

It's early summer, so there aren't too many people here. The lifeguard looks bored. We lock up our bikes and find a spot at the far end of the beach where no one likes to sit because tall grass grows where the beach ends, and there are lots of frogs and crayfish.

Micah unzips his backpack and hands me a small box wrapped in neon-green wrapping paper. "Happy birthday," he says.

I slowly unwrap the paper, careful not to rip it. The box is white with a horse head drawn in blue pen.

"Did you draw that?" I ask.

He laughs in an embarrassed way. "You know I can't draw horses."

"I like it."

Inside, there's some folded tissue paper, which I lift out to reveal a woven friendship bracelet.

"Wow," I say. "Did you make this?"

"Of course I made it. That's our rule. Do you like it?"

I nod, turning it over in my hand. "Thank you." He chose all my favorite colors: purple, blue, and green. When we were younger, we made a pact that we had to make whatever presents we gave each other. I know this was partly Micah's idea because he felt bad for me and didn't want me to feel like I had to spend money on him. I like our tradition, though. It makes all of our presents more special.

"So what are you going to do all summer?" Micah asks as he helps me tie the bracelet around my wrist.

I shrug. "Probably help my parents out with gardening chores, and find some babysitting jobs."

"Ugh. Babysitting. Not the Grayson twins, I hope."

"They live the closest."

"Those kids are horrors, though. Remember that time they tied you up and then wouldn't let you go?"

"They have boundary issues."

"They have life issues."

"At least their dad pays well."

"Well, if you take a job with them, tell me and I'll come help you."

"I can't afford to split the money. Sorry."

"I'll do it for free! That's how good a friend I am."

"You just want them to tie me up so you can laugh and take a picture."

"You don't know me at all!" He makes a fake offended face.

"Fine. You can come. Maybe you can teach them some manners."

"Exactly."

We lean back on the sand and look up at the sky. There isn't a single cloud up there, just blue, blue, blue forever.

When we're too hot, we walk to the shoreline and stand up to our ankles in the water.

"Too bad we didn't think to bring our bathing suits," I say.

"Who needs bathing suits?" Micah starts to wade into the water.

"We don't even have towels!"

"We have the sun! Come on!"

We race to see who can go under first. Micah always wins because I hate the ice rush. But I can't be outdone, so I force my head under. Beneath the water, the world feels completely different. The echoey sound of the water surrounds me, and I open my eyes.

Micah swims over to me and waves as we hold our

breath. I move my hands through the water to keep myself under, and my hair dances out around me. Micah makes a funny face, then blows bubbles at me. "Can you hear me?" he yells, but it sounds all distorted and strange. I pop my head up and gulp fresh air.

"I won!" Micah says.

I splash him and go back under and swim away from shore, out to where the rope line is. I'm going to be the first to touch it this time. As I push my arms through the water, it feels like I'm swimming through another world. Underneath me, I can see the sandy bottom, with a few rocks. Above me, the sun shines on the surface, making it look like a ripply window. The underwater sound echoes through my ears in a peaceful way, and it feels as though, for this brief moment, this is all there is and I am the only one here. Ahead, I make out the rope line and swim toward it, just as I feel a hand on my foot, pulling me back. I cough and breathe water and have to break the surface.

"Hey!" I say, sputtering.

Micah laughs and swims past me.

"Cheater! That doesn't count!"

I cough again. My throat and nose sting from the water going down the wrong way. I swim as fast as I can, but I can't catch Micah. He grabs the line and lifts it up a little, smiling. He doesn't even have to say *I win*.

The lifeguard blows her whistle at him.

"Hands off the line!"

"Sorry!" he calls at her. "Sorry not sorry," he says to me as I swim up to him. He grins.

"You're a jerk," I say.

We float on our backs and squint up at the sky.

"Wouldn't it be great if life could always be this easy?" Micah asks.

"Yeah," I say. "Imagine if I didn't have to get a summer job and we didn't have any chores, and we could just come here every day all summer."

"Do you think we'd get bored?"

"No way. We could swim, sleep, have picnics. Maybe get a boat . . ."

"How would we get a boat?"

"Maybe we'd inherit money from some long-lost rich aunt we never knew existed. And we'd never have to work a day in our lives."

I think of all the relatives I know. I'm pretty sure none of them has a secret stash of money.

"Or maybe we could just win the lottery," I say.

"I watched a show about people who won the lottery, and they all ended up miserable and poor."

"What? That's crazy. If I won the lottery, I'd be so happy. I could pay off my parents' mortgage and give them enough money so they could quit their jobs. And then I'd buy my own house, with a big barn with wood floors for Rainbow."

"Yeah, you could buy him one of those fancy blankets horses wear for the winter!"

"Only he wouldn't need it because the barn would be heated."

"Right! And he'd have an indoor riding ring, and he wouldn't have to go out all winter unless he wanted to, and that's when he'd wear his fancy coat."

"Exactly." I picture Rainbow in a fur-lined horse blanket and golden halter. He looks ridiculous. "What about you? What would you do if you won the lottery?"

Micah thinks for a minute. "I guess I'd pay off your parents' mortgage and buy you a house and a barn for Rainbow."

Micah always says selfless things like this. I wish I had thought of saying something I would get for him.

We're quiet for a while after that, both floating on our backs, slowly turning in the water.

"If there were clouds in the sky, this would feel like a scene in a movie where we say what we see and argue about which animal the clouds look like," Micah says.

I picture us in our own movie and wonder what the plot would be. Two bored friends doesn't seem like much of a blockbuster.

"I see a bluebird," I say. "The color of the sky."

"No, it's a sky-blue whale," Micah argues.

"A blue pony. With a blue mane."

"They have to be real things," Micah says. "That are really blue."

That ends our game because I can't think of any other animals that are blue like the sky.

We swim to shore and lie on our stomachs to let the sun dry our backs, then flip over to dry the other side.

"Do you think being eighth-graders will change everything?" I ask. "What if we don't have any of the same classes together? What if all our friends get divided up?"

"You really think not being in classes together will change things?" He sounds surprised and disappointed, so I don't tell him that I *do* think it could. What if Micah meets someone new? Someone more interesting than me. What if he gets a girlfriend?

He reaches over and takes my hand, as if he can read my thoughts. "I'll never leave you," he says. "Together forever. No matter what." He squeezes my fingers tight, and I squeeze back.

I concentrate on his hand in mine, wishing my heart would feel like a hummingbird trapped in my chest again, like when we were six.

But it doesn't.

If I would let him, Micah would be my boyfriend. He used to try to kiss me sometimes, but I finally told him to stop. I don't have those kinds of feelings for him. Or any boy. I never have, at least not since that time we got engaged under the lilac bushes. It's something I've only told him once, last winter, when he tried to kiss me at midnight on New Year's Eve.

"You don't like *any* boys?" he asked.

I shook my head. "I don't think so."

He was quiet for a minute, studying my face. "Does that mean you —?" He paused, looking awkward. "Does that mean you like girls?"

I shrugged. I wasn't sure about that. "I guess I don't know how I feel at all," I said.

He nodded and then got quiet for a while. "It's OK," he said finally. "This stuff is confusing." And that was the end of the conversation.

But sometimes, like now, the issue comes back silently. And silently, we let it slip back away.

ϾϿ Chapter Four ϾϿ

"The Townsends stopped by today to return my pie plate," my mom tells me when I get home that afternoon. "They also wanted to see you," she says. She looks a little sheepish, so I bet this can't be good.

"Me?"

"I know you have your heart set on getting more babysitting hours, but the Townsends have an offer I think you should consider."

"What is it?"

"Well, the way they explained it is that they moved here to start a farm, of sorts, but they have a summer home on the lake up in Northfield and want to spend most of their time there this summer, only now they have several animals that need caring for." She rolls her eyes disapprovingly. "And they're looking for someone to tend the animals while they're at their lake house."

"Me?"

"They'll pay you."

"How much?"

"I don't know, but they certainly seem like they could afford something reasonable. If you want the job, you should get over there and let them know before someone else takes it."

Lately my mom has been so moody and abrupt. Especially when we talk about anything that has to do with money.

I think about the Grayson kids and their horrible pranks. About how their house smells weird and their little dog wipes his bum on the rug because, according to the twins, he's too fat to clean himself there, and how the food the parents leave for me to make for dinner always makes me feel sick after, no matter what it is.

"I'll take it," I say. "Do I just walk over and tell them?"

"I should think so."

I slip my flip-flops on and cross the street. The driveway still smells like new, hot tar, and I imagine that for the rest of my life, when I smell this smell, it will remind me of the house that took away our field.

The front steps to the house are made of beautiful chiseled stones that they probably took from the field and that were never meant to be chiseled. Or stepped on.

A dog comes out of nowhere on the other side of the glass door and leaps against it at me, barking ferociously. Luckily it's a small dog, so he can't break the glass.

"Chablis!" a voice yells. "Stop that racket!"

Mr. Townsend appears and pulls the dog from the glass to open the door.

The dog jumps against Mr. Townsend's legs and scratches her front paws against him so he picks her up. She's white and fluffy, with big black eyes that have gross eye gunk in them.

"Raquel, right?" he asks.

"Rachel," I say.

"Oh, right. Are you here about the pet-sitting job?"

The term sounds so funny. I picture Chablis trying to tie me up like the Grayson twins did and grin. "Yes," I say.

Another little dog that looks like a much older version of Chablis only darker in color wanders over to us and also scratches at Mr. Townsend's leg. "Oh, Malbec, I can't hold you, too." He looks at me. "Would you mind?"

I pick up the little dog and hold it the way Mr.

Townsend is holding Chablis. The minute he's near my face, I nearly gag. He smells terrible, especially his breath.

Mr. Townsend sees me make a face. "I know — the old thing smells like death," he says. "We'll be taking the dogs to the lake with us, of course, so you don't need to worry about these little stinkers." It's an insult, but he says it in a sweet way, like they could smell twenty times worse and he would still love them.

We set the dogs down and go out a back door. We stop at the new horse barn first, where two beautiful big horses stand patiently in the shade. "This is Ben and Gil," Mr. Townsend says. "They're retired workhorses. Aren't they gorgeous? The old farmer we got them from was sad to see them go, but they did their time and need a nice place to be put to pasture. We'll spoil them and give them a happy end of life."

I reach out my hand, and Ben gently nuzzles my fingers, looking for a treat.

"We have apples and carrots in the fridge," Mr. Townsend says. "Let me show you."

I follow him into a third stall, which they have set up as a tack room, and he shows me how to measure the grain, then points out a mini fridge stocked with apples and carrots. I think these must be the only horses in the country that have their own mini fridge stocked with treats. Poor Rainbow. I'm glad he doesn't know what he's missing.

Mr. Townsend takes me to visit the rest of the animals and gives me instructions on how to feed them. There are two goats named Agatha and Christie; a bunch of chickens; two sheep called Ewe and Me, which Mr. Townsend thinks are the funniest names ever; a pig called Lucy, named after his sister-in-law whom he hates; and a baby steer named Ferdinand. "After Greer gave the dogs those ridiculous wine names, I insisted I got to name all the new guys," he says. "I think I did a pretty great job, no?"

I nod and pet Ferdinand's head.

"This one we saved from being veal!" he says happily, holding his hand out for the little steer to lick. "He's on the young side, so he still needs formula. But at least he doesn't need a bottle!" He shows me how to mix a white powder with water in a metal bucket. We bring it over to the little guy. His big, gentle eyes look up at me hopefully.

"Here," Mr. Townsend says, handing me the bucket. "You give it to him. I want you two to become friends!"

I place the bucket in front of Ferdinand, and he greedily sucks up all the milk, then noses the bucket across the ground until he figures out it really is empty. Meanwhile, Mr. Townsend has gone off to get a lead line and halter, which he slips over Ferdinand's head. "Now, I know this is going to sound silly," he says, adjusting the halter. "But we'd like you to take him for a walk around the property every day. We want him to get used to people and not be the kind of steer that chases people around and intimidates them."

He hands me the lead and says, "Give it a try."

Ferdinand butts me with his head as if to say, "Come on, let's go!" We walk around the farmyard, Ferdinand constantly butting me. "He thinks he's a goat," I say, trying to dodge him.

Mr. Townsend laughs. "He really likes you! I think this is a match made in heaven."

Ferdinand looks up at me and blinks his pretty, long lashes until I pet him. I think he must be smiling, as much as a steer can smile, anyway.

"Did you save all of these animals?" I ask Mr. Townsend.

"Well, I wouldn't say *saved,* but I suppose some were headed to a faster death, yes. The chickens are laying hens, but if things go well, we'll get some meat birds. And we're raising the pig for meat as well, so don't get too attached to her. That's why I named her after my sister-in-law." He elbows me and smirks.

Raising animals to eat is pretty common around

here, but I'm glad my parents never wanted to. Even if you try not to get attached, I bet it's hard.

"Greer thinks she'd like to shear the sheep and learn how to spin wool and knit, but I won't hold my breath on that one. And the goats . . . well, we just think they're fun to watch. I suppose someday we could add a female and milk her, but I'm not much of a fan of goat's milk. I'm partial to chèvre, though, so who knows! Maybe I'll become a cheese maker!"

When Mr. Townsend finishes showing me how to do the rest of the chores, he asks me if I still want the job and says they'll pay me minimum wage. This is a little surprising, given that it seems they could afford much more. But when I think of Ferdinand's sweet face and realize how much nicer it will be to see than the Grayson twins, I say yes.

"Terrific!" Mr. Townsend says, patting me on the back. "We'll need you Monday through Friday. Greer and I will come back here on weekends since the lake is too crowded with tourists then, anyway."

We shake hands, and I officially have a summer job.

When I get home, my mom is waiting for me and I tell her the news. She makes an angry face when I say how much they'll pay me. "That's how the rich stay rich," she says, disgusted.

"They seem like nice people," I tell her.

She scoffs when I describe walking Ferdinand. "Whoever heard of such a thing?" she asks. "Honestly."

"They saved him from being veal," I tell her. I don't think I've ever had veal before, but now I know I never will. How could anyone eat a baby animal?

"Mr. Townsend said we could have their extra eggs," I add, hoping this will make her feel better. "They only use one dozen per week, so if I collect more than that, I can bring them home."

"How generous," my mom says sarcastically.

I get the feeling there is nothing I can say about our new neighbors that will make my mom happy. "I thought you wanted me to take this job," I say.

She sighs and touches the top of my head, something she's done since I was little. "I do, honey. I'm sorry. I've just got a lot on my mind, and it makes me grumpy. This will be a great job for you." But she says it in a distanced way, as if her mind is already on something else — some worry she doesn't talk about but that shows on her face and in the tense way she seems to hold herself all the time now.

"Mom," I ask as she slips her hand from my head, "have you heard from the school yet?"

It's a touchy subject, asking about work. Until a year ago, she was the high-school librarian, but the town didn't pass the school budget and they cut her position. Now she works part-time for the same real-estate company as my dad, doing filing and things, but it makes her sad. Plus the school gave good family health benefits and my dad's job doesn't, so it's even more stressful. A group of parents got together to try to petition to get her job back, but so far they haven't had any luck. She keeps hoping that if the economy gets better, maybe people will be more willing to vote for the budget again. But the economy just keeps getting worse.

"No news yet," my mom says, shuffling bills and papers spread across the messy dining-room table.

I wish I hadn't asked.

"I'll give you my earnings from the Townsends," I say. "To help out."

She pauses and smiles at me. "Thanks, honey. But you keep it. We'll manage."

We'll manage is something my parents say a lot. But lately when they say it, they don't sound too convincing.

⤳ Chapter Five ↫

On Monday morning, I take care of Rainbow, then walk over to the Townsends' house to start my summer job. The dew on the grass seeps into my sneakers, and my feet are soaked and uncomfortable by the time I reach the horse barn.

Ben and Gil's horsey smell greets me as soon as I get close. It's much stronger than Rainbow's. Maybe because there are two of them and they are at least twice his size. I don't mind it, really. Horses have a certain comforting smell, like hay breath and warm fur. Ben and Gil snuffle at me and shake their heads hello. I measure their grain and put it into their buckets. While they eat, I go through the corral and open their stall doors so they can go out to the pasture, then fill their trough with water. They stay inside for a bit, still busy licking their grain buckets clean. They flick their tails at the summer flies and lift their feet to shift their weight. They're so quiet and peaceful. I think Mr. Townsend is right that they're happy with their retirement. They're certainly lucky to end up here, in this fancy barn with wooden floors and their own refrigerator filled with treats.

When Ben and Gil wander outside, I go into their stalls and shovel out their manure. There's a place behind the barn to make a manure pile, which Mr. Townsend said will make great fertilizer. But they don't have a garden yet, so I'm not sure what he plans to fertilize.

Next I visit the goats. They look like wise old men, with their serious eyes and long beards. "Hi, Agatha. Hi, Christie," I say. It feels a little strange to call boy goats female names. Mr. Townsend said he'd had to live with being called Bev all his life, so he figured a goat could handle it. Besides, people shouldn't assign gender roles to animals. "Or people," I said, without thinking. Mr. Townsend grinned and smacked me on the back. "Thatta girl," he said. Which kind of did exactly that, but I didn't say anything since I could tell his heart was in the right place.

The goats are way more eager to get their food than Ben and Gil. They go "Maaaaaa" and dance in circles while they wait for me to bring their grain. Then they almost tip over their buckets pressing their noses in. The goats do not smell good, like the horses do. Their poops are little pellet-type things that Mr. Townsend said I could rake into a pile in the corner of their pen for now. I have a feeling I'm going to be learning a lot about poop on this job.

When I get to the chickens, I start to have a sinking feeling. They look at me suspiciously from their coop, like they know I'm about to take away all the eggs they're sitting on. I sprinkle a bunch of corn feed on the ground in their outdoor pen, then open the hatch to their coop. They come out slowly, marching in a little parade down the ramp. They look the same at first, but as I study them, I can see they are different sizes and move slightly differently.

The last hen out is the tiniest and looks a bit scruffy, like she's been in a fight. Mr. Townsend said he's still trying to come up with names for all of them and I was welcome to suggest some, but I'll have to get to know them all before I can decide who's named what. As soon as they're all out, I grab the wicker basket by the door to their coop and go inside. It's hot and stuffy and smells terrible. Chicken poop is definitely the worst poop so far.

I make my way to each nest, checking for eggs and

taking what I find. The eggs are still warm, and some are dirty and it's all pretty disgusting. Just as I'm about to reach for the last nest in the far corner, one of the chickens comes back through the little hatch and clucks at me. I try to step around her, but she pecks at my ankle.

"Hey!" I yell. She does it again. It doesn't hurt, but it's a little creepy. I think this one should be called Bossy.

I step past her, and she jumps up and scratches me with her feet. This time, it hurts.

I yell again and dash out of the coop, barely shutting the door before she gets out. My ankles sting and itch where she scratched me. So much for thinking chickens were cute! I put down the basket of eggs and inspect my ankles. The scratches are little, but they sting. I'm probably going to get some kind of chicken-claw disease. I rinse the cuts at the spigot at the barn and then go back to find the egg basket. I only manage to gather five, which I put in Ben and Gil's refrigerator in the carton Mr. Townsend left.

Next up is Lucy the pig, who also has her own shelter and pen farther down the hill. I prepare her feed and some water and carry the buckets down to her. Feeding Lucy is tricky because I have to heave the bucket over her fence railing and put it on a hook on the other side. Mr. Townsend said it's not safe to go into her pen because she's about as friendly as his sister-in-law and also doesn't like kids. "They're both miserable beings," he said. "Besides, who wants to step in that?" He pointed to the stinky mud Lucy seems to love.

I think every place here is pretty stinky, just in varying degrees. But it's true that this particular section is the worst. I climb up on the first rung of the fence and heave the feed bucket over. I don't hear Lucy approaching as I settle the handle onto the hook. Suddenly she's racing straight at me as if she hasn't been fed in a week. I startle and get my hand caught between the railing and the handle just as Lucy slams her body against the bucket. I yell out as pain surges up my arm, but I manage to pull my hand back. Then I fall backward off the fence and onto my butt in the dirt.

Lucy goes wild, eating the food and making snorting noises.

I get up and brush myself off. "Rude!" I yell, but Lucy could care less. She swishes her little curly tail in circles and keeps eating in a satisfied way. One whole side of her is covered with caked-on mud. I wonder how it will come off. Maybe she rolls around and gives herself a dust bath, like Rainbow does sometimes. I hope so, because I sure don't want to have to brush it off her, especially not for minimum wage!

Every few seconds, she lifts her head from the feed bucket and gives me the evil eye. I wonder why she doesn't like people. I bet she knows her days are numbered and how unfair that is. Even though she's awful, I feel sorry for her. Maybe if I'm really, really sweet to her, the two of us can become friends and she'll be nicer and Mr. Townsend will realize she's a good pet and won't want to raise her for meat after all. I decide this is going to be my mission for the summer.

I find Ewe and Me standing together in a circle in their pen. Because one is black and one is white, they remind of me of the yin-yang symbol. I think those would have been way better names for them. They come over to say hello when I get closer with their feed. They don't go nuts like the goats; they just *baaa* sweetly and sniff the air.

Finally, it's time to tend to Ferdinand. I saved him for last since he is the cutest. I mix his formula in the barn, then go to his little hutch, which looks like an igloo. It's a special design made for young steer to keep warm and dry. I've seen them at lots of other farms and always wondered what they were. His eyes are so big and dear, and his eyelashes so long, it's hard to believe he's not some stuffed animal with exaggerated features to make him look even cuter than the real thing. How could someone kill and eat him? He sticks out his tongue when he sees the pail, eager to slurp up the milk. When he's done, I hook on his little halter and leash and take him for a walk around the property. I rub his soft head and try to train him not to nudge me, even though it seems like he's just trying to say, "Walk faster!"

As we walk around the property, I try to remember what it looked like before all this was here. When it was still our special place to ride Rainbow in the summer and go sledding in the winter. I used to know every bump and big rock and where the dips in the land fell. We made jumps out of small rises in the land to sled over, having contests to see who could get the most air on a jump. Micah usually lost. He's always been pretty cautious. I think the only time he won was when he misjudged a ramp we built. Ivy is notorious for making the ramps too steep so you go flying in the air and crash. I guess Micah and I were getting too old to play in the snow anymore anyway, but it still feels sad that we don't have a choice.

After I finish gathering the empty feed buckets and cleaning them out for the next feeding, I go back home. But instead of going inside, I walk out back to find

Rainbow, who is happily grazing on the lawn. My mom says he's the best lawn mower around because he mows the lawn *and* fertilizes it. But my dad says it's gross and backyards are no place for horse poop. Micah and I call the droppings meadow muffins. Once we nearly convinced Ivy to eat one, but our consciences got the better of us and we finally told her what they were. She cried and told my mom, who made me and Micah clean up all the muffins.

Rainbow lifts his head when he sees me, and I rub his ears. He licks my hand, looking for a treat, then seems to smell all the other animals on me and sniffs harder.

"There's a whole menagerie across the road," I tell him. "You could make all kinds of friends. But I don't think the Townsends would like me taking you over there." I describe the chickens and Lucy and sweet little Ferdinand while Rainbow pulls at the grass and grinds it with his teeth. I pet his dusty coat and braid his mane, even though I don't have anything to tie it with.

"You look very pretty," I say.

He snuffles and keeps eating, swishing his tail at the flies.

The back screen door creaks open, and my mom calls out, "How'd it go, Rach?"

"Fine!" I call back.

She comes out to join us and stands on the other side of Rainbow, petting him gently.

"I don't like the chickens," I tell her. I show her my ankle, and she makes a face.

"We should get some peroxide on that. Does it hurt?"

I shrug. "It's really not the best job in the world. But I like Ferdinand."

"Sounds cute. Though you've got to admit the idea of walking a cow on a leash to make him tame is a bit ridiculous."

"I think it's sweet," I say. "The Townsends mean well."

"I suppose. Must be nice to be able to have those kinds of hobbies, huh?"

"Yeah."

My mom looks up at our house, which needs painting, and over at the lawn that needs mowing, despite Rainbow's efforts. It seems like all she does is worry about what needs to get done around here and what bills need to be paid.

"Do you need me to do anything today?" I ask. "I don't have to go back to do evening chores until five or so."

She smiles at me. "No, hon. You should go do something fun with Micah. Use that new bike of yours. And it wouldn't kill you to include Ivy, if you can bear it. Most of her friends are at summer camp, and I'm going to work with your father later, so I can't entertain her."

"OK," I say.

"Good girl." She pats Rainbow on the behind and starts toward the garden. "I'm going to do a little weeding before work," she says.

I should go help her, I know it, but I sense she wants to be alone. She has that sad feeling about her that she gets sometimes, and I know it means she needs her space.

She opens the garden gate slowly and latches it behind her, then bends over and starts pulling weeds from the row of tomato plants. Sometimes when I help her, she hums lullabies she used to sing to me when I was little and I sing along, making up words for the parts I can't remember, as we inch our way down the rows of vegetables, pulling up weeds that will just be back tomorrow. I wish my singing would help her feel better now, but I can tell by the way she didn't ask for company that today lullabies won't help.

᠍ Chapter Six ᠍

Ivy seems shocked when I invite her to come to the beach with me and Micah. She grabs her old bike from the garage and leads the way. Her bike makes clanking noises every so often, and the brakes squeal when she uses them. She must have spent all her free time fixing mine up and ignoring her own. She may be a pain most of the time, but I realize how thoughtful it was of her to make sure my bike felt like new. Even though Ivy is only eight, I think she's kind of a mechanical genius. She's fixed the toaster, our ancient DVD player, and even the ice maker in the freezer. She loves to take things apart to see how they work. When something's broken, it seems all she has to do is stare at it a few minutes, study the mechanics of it, and then boom! She knows exactly why the thing is broken.

At Micah's, Ivy hops off her bike and runs to the door before I can even get my kickstand down.

"Micah!" she yells as she knocks excitedly.

Mr. Sasaki opens the door.

"Hey, Ivy, what's up?"

"We're going to the beach!"

"Yeah, Micah told me. I made you guys some cookies to take. Come on in and we'll pack 'em up."

Micah's dad is always doing thoughtful stuff like making cookies. Micah's mom works in sales for a pharmaceutical company and travels a lot. I almost never see her because when she is home, they have family "quality" time and Micah isn't allowed to have friends over.

"Hi," Micah says when I follow Ivy inside. He's sitting at the kitchen counter, holding a sneaker and trying to get a knot out of the laces. He finally uses his teeth to pull it loose.

"Gross!" Ivy says, impressed.

"Micah, think about all the places those laces have been," his dad says.

"Spicy," Micah says.

Mr. Sasaki looks at me and rolls his eyes. "I thought we agreed you were going to work on teaching this kid some life skills," he says to me.

"Rachel's going to teach me how to be a farmer!" Micah says, finally pulling the knot loose.

"Oh, yeah?"

"She got a job taking care of the animals at the new house. She has to feed them all and walk a baby cow on a leash!"

"It's a steer," I correct him.

"What's the difference?" Micah asks.

"A cow is a girl."

"Well, whatever, it's still silly."

"That's a big responsibility," Mr. Sasaki says to me.

I shrug. "I only started today, but it doesn't seem too hard."

"I wish someone else around here would get a job." This time Micah rolls his eyes.

"There's an opening for taking care of the Grayson twins," I say, just to annoy him.

"I'm not sure Micah could handle those two," his dad says.

"I'm standing right here," Micah says. "And I could totally handle them. I just don't choose to."

"Can't blame you," Ivy says. "I heard they set their backyard playhouse on fire, and when the firefighters came, they discovered a bunch of Barbies tied up in there, like the twins were pretending to burn people alive."

"Wow," Micah's dad says.

"Twenty years from now, when they're in the news for some scary crime, we'll be able to say we knew them," Micah says.

"I'm not sure I'd want to admit that," I say. "Maybe you *should* babysit them so you can be a positive influence on them and keep them from going to jail."

"Now, *that's* a big responsibility," Ivy says.

"All right, you guys, enough of that," Mr. Sasaki says. "Go to the beach and have fun. And wear your bike helmets!"

We bike to the beach and find our usual spot at the far end. Ivy throws her bag on the sand and doesn't even bother to lay her towel out before kicking off her sneakers, stripping to her suit, and dashing into the water.

"Thanks for letting her come with us," I say. "She's kind of bummed she couldn't go to camp."

"No problem," Micah says, looking away from me. Whenever I hint at money problems, he puts this weird distance between us. I think it makes him feel uncomfortable that he doesn't have to worry about money like I do. When he goes out to dinner, he can order whatever he wants. He doesn't even have to look at the prices. I can't even remember the last time my family went out to eat.

Micah takes his towel out of his backpack and spreads it neatly on the sand. He places his sneakers and clothes next to his pack just so. "I'm going in," he says.

"Be there in a sec."

I spread my towel next to his, then pull off my shorts and T-shirt. My mom bought me a bathing suit at our local thrift store. All the poor kids shop there, and some of the rich kids who want to look "original" and not wear whatever the latest brand is you're supposed to be wearing. I admit I looked at the label to see if it was something I might recognize from the conversations I've overheard at school. I don't know this brand. It's a plain green one-piece with a white stripe down the right side. Boring, but not horrible. And nothing that will make me stand out, I hope. I made sure it still had its original sale tags on it because wearing someone else's old clothes is weird enough but a used bathing suit is the worst, like wearing someone else's underwear.

Micah and Ivy are already way out at the rope line by the time I manage to get up to my waist.

"C'mon, wimpy!" Ivy yells, splashing toward me.

I take a huge breath and dive under, just to show

her I'm not a wimp. The cold water wraps around me and chills my scalp. I force myself to stay under and swim toward them. The familiar underwater silence surrounds me. I open my eyes and swim until I need air. When I surface, I'm just a few yards from them.

"Let's play Clueless," Ivy says. "Rachel, you're It."

"I hate being It." Clueless is something the three of us invented when Ivy was really little. It was fun when she was tiny because she could never tell what Micah and I were saying and she loved being It.

"Oh well," Ivy says happily. "Count to three and dive under."

I count to three, and we all dip under the water. Micah and Ivy are close together, a few feet away from me. They begin to have a conversation and don't stop until they need a breath.

We pop out of the water.

"Well?" Ivy says. "What were we saying?"

"I have no clue," I say.

"Don't be a sore sport."

"Poor sport."

"That, either."

"I really don't know what you were saying," I tell her. "I promise."

"Come three inches closer, then," Ivy says, all giddy. The goal is to figure out what they're saying before they can reach out and touch me.

We all bob under again and this time I can hear their voices, but they're still muffled and strange sounding.

We pop up. "Something about bikes?" I figure it's a good guess because that's pretty much all Ivy ever wants to talk about.

"Nope!" she says. They both swim a few inches closer, and we go under again.

"Blah blah me moo," Ivy says.

"Wee wee wahhh," Micah replies.

We pop up. "Something about cars?" I guess.

"Noooo!" Ivy says.

They both swim closer and are almost in reach.

"Last chance," Micah says before we all dive under again.

I think I hear Ivy say the word *cow*. It sounds like a question. And then Micah clearly says something is for dogs.

We pop up. "Have you ever walked a cow? Leashes are for dogs!" I say.

They look at each other. "Close enough?" Micah asks.

"I guess," Ivy says.

"You're It, Ivy!" I say.

"I wish this place had a dock or something to jump off," Ivy says. "It's kind of boring here."

"They should at least allow floats," Micah says.

"Yeah! That would be cool."

"What would be cool?" Sam, a friend from school, swims over to us. She looks different with her hair all wet and plastered to her face. She already has a tan.

"Hey, Sam," Micah says. "We were just wishing there was more stuff to do here."

Another girl swims over to us. "This is Sierra," Sam says. "She's new."

"Hey," she says. She has a smiley face drawn on her cheek.

"Where are you from?" Micah asks.

"Connecticut."

"Why do you have a smiley face on your cheek?" Ivy asks.

Sierra juts her cheek toward Ivy. "It's a clown," she says. "Check out his nose."

Ivy leans forward. "Is that a . . . pimple?" she asks.

"Yeah," Sierra says. "I figured if I have to have this big ugly thing on my face, I may as well make the most of it."

"That's funny!" Ivy says.

"Wow," Micah says.

"Hi, I'm Rachel," I say when she finally turns my way.

The new girl is pretty. She has light-brown skin and eyes that sparkle when she smiles.

"I'm Micah," Micah says.

"That's an interesting name," Sierra says, swimming closer.

"Yours, too."

They stare at each other in a funny way.

Sam rolls her eyes.

"Sierra, stop flirting already. Sheesh. Also, Micah and Rachel are an item, so don't go there."

Ivy's mouth drops open. "You're an item?"

Micah looks at me uncomfortably.

"We're just friends," I say.

"Oh, please," Sam says. "Everyone knows you've been in love since, like, kindergarten."

Ivy giggles. "That's true, Rach."

Sierra twirls in a circle. "I was just being friendly. Everyone says I'm a flirt, but I'm not. That's cute you've been together since you were little." She smiles at me, and my heart flutters in a funny way. I glance over at Micah, who looks hurt and curious at the same time.

"We're just friends," Micah confirms. "Really."

"Whatever you say," Sam says. She does a backward somersault in the water. "Who wants to play a game?"

"Me!" Ivy yells.

"I'm getting out," I say. "It's too cold. Nice to meet you."

Sierra waves and dives under the water and does a handstand.

When she pops back up again, Ivy points out that her clown is running. Black ink drips down the side of her face.

"Oooh, now it's a horror clown!" Sierra says.

I swim away from the group. They're already laughing without me before I reach the shore. I realize they're playing Clueless. We've never played it with anyone else before. They keep going underwater, then popping up again and laughing like crazy. I wrap my towel tight around me. As they swim closer and closer to Micah, I get the feeling he's purposefully guessing wrong so Sierra can tag him. Or Sam. It makes me feel so angry and sad and I don't understand why. It's kind of like I'm watching people take something that I thought belonged to me.

I could solve all of this by asking him out. I know he would say yes. But that wouldn't be right. I love him, but I don't *love* him. I wonder how long we can last like this before he finds someone who wants to be more than friends. I turn his bracelet on my wrist and imagine him making it for me, choosing the colors and tying knot after knot to make the pattern. Plenty of people stay friends when they start dating other people, I tell myself. It will be fine.

I lean back on my towel and squint up at the sky. Today it's filled with puffy white clouds and I can make out all kinds of shapes, but there's no one here to name them with. I close my eyes and concentrate on the sun slowly drying my bathing suit. Every few minutes, I hear the group laughing and I feel jealous. But I stay on the shore, thinking about Micah and our friendship, and wish for the hundredth time that I could feel the same way about him as I am pretty sure he feels about me. Or did feel, until he met Sierra.

"Rachel, wake up!" Ivy yells. "Oooooh, Mom is going to kill you."

"What?" I sit up and feel dizzy.

"You were sound asleep, so we left you alone," Micah says. "We didn't realize you didn't have any sunblock on."

"That's why Mom always says to put it on before we leave, or we'll forget!" Ivy says, a worried look on her face.

My arms and legs are lobster red. "Oh, no," I say. I press my thigh with my finger, and the spot turns white, then bright-red again.

"That's gonna hurt," Sam says.

She and Sierra both stand over me.

"I think I have some aloe gel in my bag," Sierra says. "I'll go get it." She skips away down the beach.

"How long was I asleep?" I ask.

"I dunno," Micah says. "A while, I guess?"

"Seriously? Why would you let me sleep?"

"We were playing our game," Ivy says. "We aren't responsible for you."

I touch my cheeks and can tell my face is going to be burnt to a crisp, too. "Thanks a lot."

"Sorry," Micah says.

Sierra returns with a tube of bright-green stuff. "Here," she says. "Rub it all over, and it will help soothe the burn."

I squeeze some out and rub it all over my burned skin. It stings a little just to touch.

"I should go home," I say.

Micah nods.

"Can I stay with Micah?" Ivy asks.

They aren't coming with me?

"I don't mind," Micah says.

That lost, sad feeling comes over me again.

"Oh," I say. "OK. Thanks."

I slip my shorts on and gather my things and leave.

At my bike, I try to put my T-shirt on but it hurts too much on my shoulders, so I stuff it in my bag and wrap the straps around the handlebars since there's no way I can wear it on my burnt shoulders. The ride home is lonely without Ivy telling jokes or Micah singing and trying to pass me whenever there aren't any cars coming. I pedal slowly, wishing I'd just stayed in the water and played with them. Why do I have to be so sensitive? That's what my mom always says. *You're too sensitive, Rachel.* She says it every time I get upset about anything. I used to get mad at her because she made me feel like she didn't care about something that was important to me. But maybe she was right. Maybe whatever I was upset about wasn't all that important.

Like, maybe Sierra *was* just being friendly and maybe no one cares if Micah and I are friends or not and maybe no one would care about who I might like or not like.

When I reach my house, my dad's van is still in the driveway, which seems strange since my mom said they were both going to work today. I park my bike and start to go inside when I hear shouting.

"It does matter, Paul!" my mom yells. "Things have to get paid on time. They put the due dates on bills for a reason!"

"There's a grace period," my dad says. "Calm down. Everything will be fine."

"You say that, but that doesn't make it true. We can't have a grace period indefinitely. Sooner or later, we're going to have to figure out a way to pay."

"We'll get there," my dad says. "Yelling at me and acting like a . . . like this all the time isn't going to help."

"Acting like a what?" my mom says.

"Just forget it."

Footsteps come closer to the front door, so I quickly run back to my bike and pretend I just got here.

My dad swings open the door and stomps out. He doesn't even see me as he storms to his van. He gets in and pulls out way too fast. If I'd just been pulling in the driveway, he could have hit me.

My mom yells a bad word through the screen window as she slams something into the kitchen sink. It clangs and she swears again. Until recently, my mom never yelled or swore. And certainly never called my dad names.

I go inside and find her crying in the kitchen.

"Oh, Rachel. I'm sorry. Did you hear us fighting?"

"I think the whole neighborhood might have."

She slumps onto a chair at the kitchen table, looking completely wiped out.

"Is everything OK?" I ask. "Why aren't you both at work?"

"Huh? Oh." She sighs. "The bank called and . . . we just got caught up in dealing with some money stuff."

"Why were you fighting?"

She smiles weakly at me. "It was nothing, honey. Money stuff always makes us stressed, but we'll manage."

"It didn't sound like you believed that a second ago."

She clasps her hands together, then unclasps them and sweeps away imaginary crumbs from the tabletop.

"Sometimes I overreact," she says.

It feels like a lie.

I sit down in the empty chair next to her. "Mom, I want to help out. I'll give you the money I make from the Townsends. I know it's not much, but—"

She reaches over and pats my head in her special way. "Thanks, Rach. We'll see."

We're quiet for a minute, then she looks around. "Where's Ivy?"

"She stayed at the beach with Micah."

"Why did you come home without—?" She stops and notices my lobster-red skin. "Oh, dear God, Rachel, what happened?"

She jumps up and wets a dish towel with cold water and presses it against my cheeks, arms, and shoulders. It feels so good and awful at the same time.

"I fell asleep while everyone was playing in the water. I forgot to put sunblock on when I got out."

"Oh, Ray," my mom says. "This is going to hurt for a while."

"I'm sorry," I say. I don't know why, but I start to cry. Tears slip down the sides of my face, and my chest heaves out the sadness and worry locked inside.

"Don't cry, honey. I'm not mad. I just don't want to see you in pain."

I cry harder and can't seem to stop.

"Rachel, what is it?"

"Nothing," I say, choking up more sorrow. I don't know how I could ever talk to my mom about how I feel. I don't even understand it myself, really. I'm so scared. Scared of losing Micah. Scared of my parents' money problems. Scared of being . . . different.

"I'd hug you, honey, but I'm afraid it would hurt too much."

I take deep breaths and finally settle down. "It's OK," I say, wiping my eyes. "I don't know what's wrong with me."

"Hormones," my mom says. "Maybe it's just hormones."

I guess in some way she's right, but it feels so much bigger than that.

"Did Dad go to work without you?" I ask to change the subject, even if it's no better. "He seemed pretty mad."

"He'll be all right. I just pushed him too much, is all. Your dad . . . he doesn't always take bills and things seriously and that kind of thing really stresses me out. I don't like being late on payments. Your dad's a bit more laid back about it."

"Do we owe a lot of money?" I ask.

My mom gets up and rinses the cloth with cold water again, then comes back and presses it gently against my forehead.

"A bit," she says. "But we'll manage. Like your dad says, we always do."

She doesn't sound very hopeful about this, though.

"That was nice of Micah to spend time with Ivy," my mom says. "He's such a sweet boy."

She says it in that way that suggests he is the perfect boy. The perfect boyfriend, that is.

I picture Micah again with Sam and Sierra and how the way they were together isn't like the way we used to be with friends. Now it's clear who the girls are and who the boy is and we're not just a bunch of friends—we're potential "interests." And having fun and fooling around isn't just playing anymore—it's flirting. And I don't want it to be. I don't want it all to change.

I get up from the table and rinse the cloth with cold water again. "I'm going to go lie down until I have to do chores at the Townsends," I say.

"All right, honey. Let me know if you need anything. I guess I'm not working at the office today after all. Unless your dad comes back to get me."

"He'll come back, Mom," I say. "He always does."

"I know."

I leave her sitting at the kitchen table, wiping away invisible crumbs. I wish it was as easy to wipe away all her worries.

⟨ Chapter Seven ⟩

Ben and Gil seem extra happy to see me when I open their stable doors and let them in to eat their dinner. When they're done, they wander back into the corral to watch me finish my chores. They stand apart just enough to swish their tails against each other to shoo away the flies they can't reach themselves. "What good friends you are," I tell them. They stare back in their quiet, gentle way.

The chickens race toward me when I spread their feed around in their pen. I'm glad I only have to collect eggs once a day. The little scruffy chicken stands outside the frenzy. I toss a handful of feed in her direction, but then all the others scramble that way and leave her out of the group again. I keep trying to toss feed to her, but the other chickens seem determined not to let her eat. Eventually they settle down in one area because I've tossed so much feed everywhere that they can't be in all the places at once, and the little one finally gets some food. I decide to call her Bashful.

"Poor thing," I tell her. "Why are they so mean to you?"

"Because they're all bullies," a fake baby voice says behind me.

I jump a mile.

"Micah! You scared me!"

"How's the sunburn?" he asks.

"Painful. How are Sam and Sierra?"

"You're not going to ask about Ivy?"

"I know how Ivy is. Thrilled she got to spend the afternoon with you." I sound like a jealous jerk, but I can't seem to help myself.

Micah shrugs. "They're fine," he says. "Why are you asking like that?"

"Like what?"

"In that weird tone of voice. Like you're jealous."

"Do you like them?"

"Sure. They're fine, I guess."

"I mean like them, like them. You know, like could one of them be a possible girlfriend?"

"What? No. I mean, I don't know. Why are you asking me this?"

I shrug.

"Why?" he asks again.

"A lot of people start dating by eighth grade."

"So?"

"I just wondered what will happen to us. You know. If you get a girlfriend."

He rolls his eyes. "Nothing."

I can tell he's irritated with me.

"I'm sorry I was a jerk," I tell him. "You're right. I was jealous."

"Why were you jealous? I thought you didn't want to be more than—never mind. You're really confusing me, Rachel."

We watch the chickens ignore Bashful for a while. It makes me sadder than I already am.

"I don't want to be more than friends," I finally say. "But I don't want to lose you, either. And I know that's not fair."

"You won't lose me if I get a girlfriend, all right? Do two guys stop being friends when one of them starts dating a girl? No. So why should we be different?"

We shouldn't be. But . . . "Never mind," I say. "I'm just sorry for the way I acted. OK?"

"Sure. Fine. OK."

He follows me to the barn and watches me mix Lucy's feed.

"That smells pretty disgusting," he says.

"She seems to like it." I fill a bucket of water and motion for him to carry it while I lug the feed bucket to Lucy's pen. She appears to be asleep in the shade of her shelter, so I quickly step up on the fence with the bucket and swing it over and try to settle the handle in its hook before she wakes up. She must have been faking, because the minute I step on the fence, she comes charging out of her shelter and rams her side against the fence again. I drop the bucket and fall back into Micah, who falls back onto the ground, spilling the water bucket he was carrying all over both of us. I roll off Micah into the puddle. My sunburn stings where I rubbed against him.

"Sheesh," Micah says, sitting up. "Are you OK?"

"Dumb pig." I get up and brush myself off, then reach down to pull him up. "I'll be right back. Gotta go get more water."

Micah walks over to the fence and watches Lucy. She snorts at him and goes wild eating her food before any more can seep out from under the fence.

When I return with the water, Micah is standing on the lowest rung of the fence, talking to Lucy. "You know, if you didn't body-slam Rachel when she's trying to feed you, you wouldn't lose half your food. I thought pigs were supposed to be intelligent."

She grunts at him and flicks her curlicue tail.

"She hates me," I say. "How come she's not trying to knock you down?"

"She just wanted her food."

I climb up the fence and balance next to him. Lucy steps closer, as if she's going to try slamming me off again. But then she seems to think better of it and turns away from us, farting a little with each step so a tiny bit of poop squirts out of her butt each time a hoof hits the ground.

"Wow!" Micah says.

"So gross."

Lucy turns back, and I swear she smiles a wicked smile at me.

"You sure are making it hard to be friends," I tell her.

"Why do you want to be friends?"

"I want to save her," I say.

"From what?"

"Becoming bacon. The Townsends are raising her for meat."

Micah makes a face. "I wish you hadn't told me that."

"Where do you think meat comes from?"

"I don't like thinking about it."

"Well, anyway, I bet if I can tame her, like Ferdinand, Mr. Townsend will decide to keep her for a pet."

"Hmm," Micah says.

"What?"

"That doesn't seem like a very realistic plan."

Lucy watches both of us, as if she knows what we're talking about.

"Well, it can't hurt to try," I say.

Micah follows me to the sheep pen and waits while I get their food together. "What are their names?" he asks.

"That's Me, and that's Ewe," I say, pointing.

"How come I have to be the fat one?" he asks.

"No, I mean those are their names."

"Their names are Rachel and Micah?"

"No, they're Me and Ewe."

"What?"

I realize we are now having the conversation Mr. Townsend dreamed of when he gave them these dopey names.

"That one's name is Me," I say slowly, pointing. "And that one's name is Ewe."

"No," Micah says. "Really?"

"Yup. Ewe. E-W-E. Get it?"

"Ha!"

"It's really not that funny."

He shrugs. "They're pretty cute, huh? Kind of like me and you?"

"You are the biggest dork."

"Are you talking to me or Ewe?"

"Stop!" I say, laughing.

"See? It *is* funny."

"Fine."

Micah helps me with the rest of the chores, and then we walk Ferdinand.

"Aw, you're so sweet!" Micah tells him. "I can't believe someone was going to eat you, buddy! That's terrible."

Ferdinand gums Micah's arm, leaving a trail of saliva and formula chunks.

"Ew!" Micah says. He leans over before I know what he's up to and wipes his arm on mine.

"Ow!" I say.

"Oops, forgot about the burn."

We hold up our spitty arms. "We're steer spit brothers!" he says.

"Better than blood." I grab his arm and press it gently

against mine, even though it stings. "Make a vow," I say. "Like you do when you become blood brothers."

He thinks for a minute. "I solemnly swear that we will always be together no matter what."

They are the same words we've been saying since we were six. *Always together.* But as what? Why couldn't he say *Friends forever,* like normal best friends would say?

"What?" he asks, waiting for me to promise.

"Nothing," I say. I wipe some spit off my friendship bracelet.

"Well, then, swear it."

I feel an ache in my stomach because it feels a little like a lie to say the words.

"I swear," I say.

He pulls apart from me, and we let Ferdinand lick our arms clean.

"He just ate our promise," I say.

Micah gives me a funny look. "Sometimes you say the weirdest things."

We walk all around the property, reminiscing about when it still felt like ours, and where we used to sled and make jumps.

"Nothing ever stays the same for long, does it?" he asks.

"I guess not," I say.

We walk along quietly after that, until Ferdinand gets antsy and wants to play. He head-butts Micah, and Micah starts to run with him, dodging away every time Ferdinand tries to push him.

"I don't think we're supposed to encourage that!" I call after them.

Ferdinand turns at the sound of my voice and pulls Micah toward me. When they reach me, I give Ferdinand a hug. He nudges my chest and almost knocks me over.

"Easy!" I say.

"OK, let's get him back to his pen."

Ferdinand looks sad when we leave him alone.

"Poor little guy," Micah says. "He must be so lonely."

"He has me," I say.

"Lucky." Micah looks at me and smiles, but it's kind of a sad smile and it makes me feel guilty.

"C'mon," I say. "Let's go ride bikes or something." I meant ride our bikes to someplace, but it comes out sounding more like what a little kid would say. Like we're going to go ride bikes in the driveway the way we used to, and make obstacle courses with chalk and scraps of wood for ramps. I think Micah reads my mind, but instead of making fun of me, he gets all excited and says, "Yeah!"

Back at the house, we search in the garage for some wood and make a few ramps in the driveway. Ivy comes out to see what we're doing and immediately joins in by setting up obstacles for us to bike around. For the next few hours, we feel like little kids again, and like the kind of friends we've always been until now. We whoop when we ride over jumps and make stupid sounds as we take tight corners and pop wheelies.

When my dad gets home, he parks in the grass so we can keep playing. He looks less angry than when he left. It used to be that when my parents had an argument and my dad stormed off, he'd come back with flowers for my mom, or a bag of her favorite takeout. But today he's empty-handed, which is probably a good thing because I don't think my mom would be too happy if he spent money on something frivolous.

"Been a while since you guys did this!" he says.

Micah goes over a ramp. "Hi, Mr. Gartner!" he calls.

"Nice to see you, kid," my dad calls back.

The three of us keep riding until we're too tired. Then we ditch our bikes and go out back to find Rainbow and give him clumps of grass. We pet him, and he licks my hand like he always does, as if it's his way of saying hello. He only licks mine, though—no one else's. We lie on our backs in the grass and listen to him chomp nearby and look up at the sky, now filled with puffy clouds.

"Blue whale suffering from cloud-itis," Micah says.

"It's a pony," I say. "With cotton-itis."

"You two are weird," Ivy says.

Micah reaches for my hand again, and I hope for those old hummingbirds but of course nothing happens. I reach over and hold Ivy's hand, so the three of us are connected. I lift our hands up so they can see I'm holding both.

Normally Ivy would say "ew" and pull away, but seeing that the three of us are joined together, and that she's part of the connection, she squeezes my hand instead. "Thanks for hanging out with me today, you guys," she says.

"Anytime," Micah says.

"Well," I add, "mostly. If you poop in the bathroom before I have to brush my teeth again, there will be trouble."

"Ew!" Micah says. "Ivy, that's disgusting."

Ivy giggles. "That's payback for the meadow muffins."

"Ha! I forgot all about that!" Micah elbows me. "We were so evil back then."

"It's just what siblings do," I say.

We let go of hands then and settle with our own thoughts until my mom calls us in for dinner.

After Micah leaves, I go to my room to read. Ivy comes in and sits at the end of my bed before I can open my book.

"Mom and Dad started arguing again," she says.

We listen for a minute, but I don't hear anything.

"I'm worried."

"They'll be OK," I say. "It's just about money."

"That's what I'm worried about. The money."

"What do you mean?"

"I heard Mom on the phone while you were at the Townsends'. She was talking to a bank, I think. She asked them about how to take out a second mortgage. What does that mean?"

"I don't know," I say.

"It didn't sound like a good thing. And it didn't sound like they would let her borrow more money. She started crying on the phone."

I put my book down and look out the window, trying to think of something reassuring to say.

"What happens when you can't pay your mortgage?" Ivy asks.

"I don't know. But try not to worry. Mom and Dad will figure something out."

But I'm not sure that's true. I'm not sure at all. Until recently, my mom almost never cried, and certainly not over money. I wonder how much we owe the bank, and how many hours of babysitting I could work in addition to my job at the Townsends' to help pay for the mortgage. My guess is not enough.

"Maybe I could get a job," Ivy says. "I could babysit for the evil twins."

"But you're practically the same age," I point out. "I don't think their parents would hire you."

"There has to be something I can do to help."

Her eyes water and a tear slips down her cheek, which she quickly wipes away. This is not our carefree, pain-in-the-butt, smelling-up-the-bathroom-on-purpose Ivy. This is a stressed-out, scared Ivy. Seeing her this way makes me feel a little scared, too.

"It's going to be OK," I say again. "Mom and Dad will work it out."

She nods as another tear slips down her cheek. "OK." She gets up and walks to the door. "Thanks again for today," she says. "And sorry about the sunburn."

"It's fine," I tell her.

"Today was fun, right? Other than the burn?"

"Yeah, it was."

"I wish every day could be like this, except for the Mom and Dad part."

"Me too," I say.

I listen to her shuffle down the hall to her bedroom. George pads into my room and jumps on the bed. He slowly walks up to me and stretches his nose to my face, sniffing. Then he walks in a careful circle and plops down next to my head. I rest my cheek against his soft fur and listen to his reassuring purrs until I finally fall asleep.

ᏋᏟ Chapter Eight ᏝᎧ

Sierra invited us to a party, Micah texts me the next morning. *She has a pool!*

I get that jealous feeling again. Why didn't Sierra invite me personally? She could get my number from Sam. Or even Micah. Instead of replying, I take care of Rainbow and then go over to the Townsends'.

Even though it's on the early side, it's already hot and muggy and the animals seem to move in slow motion.

When it's time to gather eggs from the chickens, I scatter their feed in their outdoor pen first, then unlatch the doors to their coop. They all shuffle out in a line. Poor Bashful staggers out last. I quickly toss some feed to her before the others can reach it.

Inside the coop, I start my egg search. Each nest has

one egg, which I carefully place in the basket. Some of them are kind of gross because they are slightly wet and I don't want to think about why, and some have a little chicken poop on them. When I get to the last nest, I pick up the egg, but it slips out of my hand and lands on the floor and cracks open. The bright-yellow yolk spreads across the floor. While I'm still wondering how the heck I'm going to clean it up, a chicken appears in the doorway, then another, and suddenly they are all attacking one another to get to the cracked egg to eat it. The biggest one pecks at me to get out of the way. A horrible urge to throw up rises in my throat, and I cover my mouth and rush outside, quickly closing the latch behind me. I nearly drop the whole basket as I run away from the coop and the sound of their feeding frenzy.

"Gross! Gross, gross!" I yell as I run to the barn. I gag as I put the disgusting eggs into the egg carton. I wash my hands under the spigot until the water numbs them. "Gross!" I yell again. "Grooooooosssss!"

Ewe and Me walk to the edge of their pen and watch me.

"They're gross!" I yell.

The sheep just stare.

"Ugh! Never mind!"

I fill Lucy's bucket with feed, then decide to try a

new approach and put her water bucket out first. She eyes me from her shelter and shows no interest as I lift the bucket over the railing and hang it on the latch. In fact, she rolls over and flicks her tail at me, as if to say, "Talk to the butt."

"Whatever," I tell her, and go back for the feed. I return quietly, watching her backside as I approach. She doesn't stir. As soon as I begin to climb onto the fence and heave the heavy bucket over, though, she grunts, gets to her feet, and stares at me.

"Just wait," I say.

She grunts again and stomps her hooves, getting ready to charge.

I quickly hook the handle into place just as she starts toward me at full speed. I jump down right before she heaves her side against the fence and tips the bucket over, spreading her food all over the ground.

"Why?" I ask as we watch it spread under the fence and out of her reach. "Micah's right. For an animal that's supposed to be smart, you sure are lacking in the brains department."

She snorts again and begins to slurp up the food. She flicks her curly tail and ignores me. When she reaches the part that's gone under the fence, she crouches down and sticks her snout under the railing pathetically.

"Dumb pig," I say again. I get a shovel and try to push the food back her way. She doesn't seem grateful at all.

I take Ferdinand for an extra-long walk and then go back home. Micah has texted me three more times about Sierra's party, saying that we need to go because everyone is going to be there.

I'll think about it, I text back.

I don't know why his texts are making me so moody. Or why I feel the need to torture him instead of just agreeing to go. Am I jealous of Sam and Sierra? But why? I guess I just don't want things to change, and I have this sinking feeling that they're about to.

Did you do chores yet? he texts back. *Want to go to the beach?*

Can't. Sunburn.

Oh.

He doesn't offer to do something else. I bet he'll go without me. I bet he'll go and hang out with Sam and Sierra. I try to think of something fun for us to do instead, but what else is there on a hot summer day? There's always the movies, but that costs money.

Maybe I could go to the beach if I wear long sleeves and a hat.

I text him back and say I want to go after all.

What about your burn? he asks.

I'll cover up.

We agree to meet at his house in an hour. As soon as Ivy finds out, she begs to go with us again and I feel too guilty to say no.

The beach is more crowded today, and I'm hot and grouchy. I wear my long-sleeve shirt into the water, which actually feels kind of soothing. We play Clueless for a while, but it gets boring pretty fast.

Micah starts to float on his back. Ivy tries, but her butt sinks and she can't stay up.

"You have to relax," I tell her. "And breathe."

She tries again but keeps sinking, so Micah and I spend the rest of the morning trying to teach her how to float. After a while, I get the impression that she knows how to do it but just likes the attention. Luckily two of her classmates show up and she leaves us to go play with them.

Micah and I stay in the water, wading in the deep at the far corner of the rope line.

"So about the party," Micah says. I knew it was only a matter of time before he brought it up.

I roll my eyes and twirl in a circle.

"C'mon," he says. "It could be fun!"

"Don't say everyone's going to be there."

"Why not?"

"Because for one thing, it's probably not true. Do you think Russell Colvak will be there? Or Maggie Wilson?"

These are two kids in our grade who no one really talks to. Maggie acts like she's still five years old. No one really knows why. People try to be nice to her, but I think people are also a little afraid of her, which is totally unfair, but sometimes people are afraid of what they don't understand. Or who. Micah and I tried to eat with her at lunch once, but her aide told us she prefers to eat alone. Russell is a boy who spends every free minute playing this strange game on his phone that he's addicted to and refuses to talk to anyone. Micah downloaded the game on his phone and we tried to play to see what was so great about it, but it made us both feel carsick, so we gave up.

"OK, well, maybe not everyone," Micah says. "But a lot of people."

"Why do you want to go so badly?"

He thinks for a minute. "I don't know, Rachel. I just do. I think it could be fun. Sierra's pool has a diving board!"

"Whoop-de-do."

"Oh, please. You know you want to try it. Why do you have to be such a snob?"

"*I'm* not the snob. Sheesh! I probably don't have the right brand bathing suit to wear."

"Sierra isn't like that, Rachel. She's nice. I mean, she invited you after you totally ignored her."

"I didn't totally ignore her!"

"Um. Yeah, you did."

I swim farther away from him.

"You have a crush on her, don't you?" I say.

"What? No! Why would you say that? You've been acting so weird lately. What's going on?"

"Nothing."

"Liar."

I sigh and float on my back, trying to figure out what my problem is. Why *do* I feel so angry with him all the time, even though he hasn't done anything wrong?

I swim back over to him. "You're right. Sorry I've been acting weird."

"Maybe the animals are stressing you out."

"Maybe," I say. I tell him about the chicken eggs to change the subject.

"That is so disgusting," he says. "Who knew chickens were cannibals?"

"Not me. I'm never eating eggs again. At least not ones from the Townsends."

"How was Lucy? Did she try to attack you again?"

"Yes. She really hates me."

"I think she hates life."

"Yeah. Well, she doesn't have the best existence in the world."

"But . . ."

"It's better than the alternative," we say at the same time.

"Hey, guys!" a voice calls from shore.

It's Sam.

Micah waves happily, so I follow his lead and do the same.

"Where's Sierra?" he asks when Sam joins us.

"She's home getting ready for the party. She said she didn't need help. You guys are going, right?"

"Definitely," Micah answers for both of us.

"How's your burn?" Sam asks me.

"It's fine. Just stings a bit still. The water feels good, though."

We talk about the summer movies we want to go to, and Micah invites Sam to come with us. I don't admit to them that I probably won't go. I pretend that it's all fine, though, and we discuss which theater is better. We have a small one at one end of town that shows artsy films and a bigger one on the other side of town that shows the blockbuster kind. The bigger one is really old, and people call it the Sticky instead of the Stickley, which is its real name. When you walk down the aisle to get to your seat, your feet stick to the floor because they never mop it. And you have to be careful and check your seat before you sit down because there could be someone's messy candy wrapper or popcorn pieces in it. But the screens are bigger, so it's more fun to see action movies there.

"One time I was walking up the aisle to go use the bathroom in the middle of a movie and my flip-flop came off because it got stuck in a wad of gum," Sam says. "I lost my balance and had to step down with my bare foot and I stepped on a gummy worm and thought it was a real worm and I screamed bloody murder and everyone in the theater shushed me at the same time. It was so embarrassing! I couldn't find my flip-flop until there was an explosion in the movie and the screen lit up the aisle a little."

"I think we were there!" Micah says. "I kind of remember that!"

"Me too!" I say. "That's so funny."

"It's funny now," Sam says. "But it was kind of horrifying at the time."

We spend the next hour or so sharing our most embarrassing stories. I always thought Sam was kind of a snob, but she seems different this summer. When our fingers turn into prunes, we decide to get out and dry off. Soon it's time to go, so we drag Ivy away from her pals and bike home. She and Micah come to the Townsends' to help me with chores, and I introduce Ivy to all my new friends and enemies. When we get Lucy her feed and water, she does her usual body-slam routine and Ivy thinks it's too funny for words.

"Boy, she really hates you, Rachel!" Ivy says.

As if to confirm this, Lucy flicks her tail and poops. Pig poop is ten times smellier than anything I've ever smelled. When the stench hits us, Ivy exaggerates, clutching her chest and falling to the ground.

"I'm dying!" she yells, rolling around and plugging her nose.

Lucy ignores us.

"She's no Wilbur, that's for sure," Ivy says. *Charlotte's Web* is one of her favorite books. I've probably read it to her four or five times.

"She's 'Some Pig,' all right," I say, quoting the words Charlotte weaves into her web to try to save Wilbur.

"'Terrific,'" Ivy says. We both laugh.

"I feel sorry for her," Micah says. "Look at her. She seems sad."

"Maybe she knows her destiny," I say.

"What do you mean?" Ivy asks.

"She's being raised for meat."

A worried look comes over Ivy's face, and I regret telling her.

"You know some farms raise animals for food," I tell her.

"I know, but . . ." Ivy looks like she's about to cry. "It's different when you know them. Maybe you could be Lucy's Fern, Rachel! Maybe you could save her!"

We all step up on the bottom rung of the fence to watch Lucy. I imagine running up to Mr. Townsend the way Fern does to her dad when he goes out to the hog house to "do away" with Wilbur. Only I don't imagine Mr. Townsend with an ax. He'll probably hire someone to come do the job. The thought of it makes me feel queasy.

Lucy flips her ears forward as she watches us, and for a minute, she does seem kind of cute. But then she scratches her hoof against the ground again, as if she's going to charge us all.

"Come on, Lucy, don't be like that," says Micah. "We were just talking about saving you!"

She tilts her head and poops again.

"Wow," Ivy says.

"Our minister says you have to love the hell out of some people," Micah says. "That should be our summer goal for Lucy."

"What does it mean?" Ivy asks.

"It means you need to love your enemies. Or people you don't like. They probably need it. When they feel loved, they won't be so awful."

"Is that really what it means?" I ask.

"It's my interpretation," Micah says.

"I like it!" Ivy says. "Lucy, I'm going to love the hell out of you, too. Maybe if we love her, she'll stop being so mean and the Townsends will feel sorry for her and save her after all. Maybe they'll love the hell out of her, too!"

"Don't say hell," I say.

"It's not a swear in this context," Micah points out.

"Whatever," I say. "Just don't get too attached."

"Let's make a pact," Ivy says, ignoring me. She reaches her hand over the fence and points it toward

Lucy, palm down. Micah reaches out and puts his hand on top of Ivy's. I place my hand on top of both.

"We solemnly swear to love the hell out of you, Lucy," Ivy says seriously. "And you should let us. Because it could save your life!"

"I promise," Micah says.

"Promise," I add.

Lucy flops over and rolls in the mud.

"I think that means she's thinking about liking us," Ivy says.

"I like your optimism," Micah tells her.

We take turns walking Ferdinand and letting him chase us around the yard. He kicks his hooves happily as he skips around, putting us all in a good mood. Micah and Ivy offer to feed the chickens since I'm still grossed out by them. I don't think Ivy and I have ever gotten along so well. She's a good kid, when she's not stinking up the bathroom on me.

Once chores are done, we go back to the house and ride our bikes in the driveway again, until Micah says he needs to go home and shower to get ready for Sierra's party. I had forgotten all about it.

"What do I wear?" I ask.

"I knew you'd change your mind!" he says, clapping

his hands together. "It's a pool party, so I assume at least a bathing suit."

"I know *that*," I say. "But . . . do I wear shorts? A sundress?"

"How should I know?" Micah says.

"That's not helpful."

"Can I go to the party?" Ivy asks.

"No," Micah and I say at the same time.

Ivy frowns.

"Sorry. It's just for people our age."

"Sounds stupid," she says.

"I think you should wear what you feel comfortable in," Micah tells me. "Just be yourself."

As he walks away, I think about that phrase. *Be yourself*. It sounds so easy, on the surface. But lately, deep down, I feel like I'm not sure what being myself really means.

ᏻ Chapter Nine ᏻ

I put my hair up in three different ways, but I hate how it looks no matter what. When I try on the one sundress I got last year, it's too tight and too short anyway. I don't feel any taller, but I guess I am. I try on every pair of shorts I own, and they all look too old and worn. Even my new bathing suit looks old.

I go downstairs and find my mom to ask her for advice. She's always been good at putting outfits together and making them look better than I ever could.

"I think what you have on looks nice, honey. I'm sure if it's a pool party, anything goes. You'll probably be in your bathing suit the whole time anyway."

I'm wearing cutoffs and an old white T-shirt—the kind that comes in a three-pack at the under-five-dollars store. It is not party wear, and she barely even looks at me, so how does she know if what I have on is OK?

"Please, Mom? Can you just come up and help me?"

She finally stops tearing lettuce for tonight's salad and really looks at me.

"Hmm. All right."

We go to my room, and she picks up all the various clothes I've discarded on the floor and lays them out on my bed, mixing and matching until she finds a combination she likes. "Try that," she says.

I haven't undressed in front of my mom for a long time, and I feel funny, especially now that I wear a bra.

"You've grown!" she says.

"Mom!" I want to crawl under the bed. "Don't say that!"

I put on the outfit and turn in a circle.

"I like it!" my mom says. "But, honey, there's a hole in the armpit and I don't think I can sew that material properly. It's too thin." She rummages through a few shirts and pulls out a pale-blue T-shirt with a tiny bird on one sleeve. I'm not sure where it came from. Probably something she grabbed for me a long time ago from the free box they put out once a year downtown near the fancy shops. All the rich people leave their kids' hand-me-downs in boxes along the sidewalk and all the not-rich people walk up and down and take things from it. I hate picturing my mom sorting through those boxes, trying to find us clothes. I remember her asking me to go with her and I said no, pretending I didn't feel well, when really I didn't want to go because I was afraid someone from school would see me.

"That looks cute!" my mom says when I slip the bird shirt over my head and adjust it so it's partly tucked in and partly not tucked in. She walks over to me and adjusts it around my waist a little more.

"There. Super cute. Now, what should we do with your hair?"

"I'm having a bad hair day," I say.

"Nonsense. Go get a brush and some hair bands and we'll give you an updo."

"Updo?"

"You'll see."

My mom brushes my hair and gets all the knots out. Having her do my hair takes me back to when I was little and she'd sing pretty songs to me while she brushed my hair after bath time. She pulls it back and does some braiding and then puts it all in place with an old barrette that has a rainbow on the tip.

"See?" she says, guiding me to the mirror. "Super cute."

It does look pretty cute. Not too fancy, and not like my mom did it for me. It's kind of messy, but in a nice way.

"Thanks, Mom," I say.

"Now just spend a little time letting everyone admire it before you jump in the pool and get your hair wet!" She pinches my side in a loving way and gives me a hug. It's so nice to have this mom back for a minute. This mom that I remember before she started getting so stressed out about money.

"Is Micah picking you up soon? Or do you have time to have some dinner with us?"

I check my phone. "He's coming in a half hour. There's going to be food at the party, I think, so I don't need dinner."

"OK," she says. "Be sure to offer to help clean up before you come home. And come find me when you get back so you can tell me all about it."

"Mom," I say. "You know Micah and I are just friends, right? That's all we'll ever be."

She smiles, like she thinks I'm not being honest with her. "We'll see," she says playfully.

"No, Mom, really." I want to tell her why I know this. That I've tried and tried to feel differently about him but

I just can't. But I don't feel ready to talk about why with her. Not until I'm really sure.

Besides, my mom looks so happy for once, I don't want to ruin the moment by getting all serious.

"Try not to be so definite about everything, Ray," she says. "Go with the flow. You never know what might happen between the two of you."

"Fine," I say.

She smacks my butt playfully and leaves me alone.

Thirty more minutes until the party. I walk over to the mirror and look at myself again. I look like me, and not me. A little taller. A little older. I turn one way and then the other, then get a hand mirror so I can see my hair from behind. *Pretty*, I allow myself to think. But then I notice a little stain on the bottom hem of my T-shirt.

Of course.

Almost pretty, I think instead.

But it will have to do.

༼ Chapter Ten ༽

"Wow," Micah says when he shows up on his bike. "How are you going to wear a bike helmet with that hairdo?"

"Really?" I ask. Sometimes Micah's practicality ruins everything.

"Sorry. I mean, you look nice!"

"Too late. Can't we just walk? It's not that far."

"I guess," he says.

"I'll give you a ride!" my dad says, giving away that he was spying on us through the screen door.

I want to scream, *This is not a date!* But I keep quiet.

"Shotgun!" Ivy calls from inside.

Were they *all* spying?

"Why are you coming?" I ask Ivy when she gets in the front seat.

"I want to see what Sierra's house looks like. And the pool."

"You're not getting out of the car," I say. "So unless the pool is in the front yard, forget seeing it."

"Be nice, Rachel," my dad says. "But yeah, Ivy, we're just dropping them off. Let's not embarrass Micah and Rachel in front of their new friend."

"You wouldn't embarrass me," Micah says, the suck-up. He's always trying to impress my parents. It drives me crazy.

"Can you just drop us off at the end of the street, Dad?" I ask.

"Oh, come on, Rachel. We aren't *that* embarrassing."

"Fine."

He leaves us at the end of the driveway at least. We walk up to the house and knock on the door. A beautiful older woman greets us. "I'm Mrs. Lloyd, but you can call me Clarissa," she says.

We introduce ourselves.

"Oh, Micah and Rachel. I've heard about you. Well, come on in. The kids are out back." She leads us through the house to the backyard. The floors in the house are newly carpeted and smell like "new house." The furniture looks like it all came from the same fancy catalog. It feels a lot like Micah's house, only newer. Micah doesn't seem to notice any of it, but I can't stop looking and fall a little behind.

One side table is covered with photos of Sierra, from when she was a baby to now. There are at least twenty of them, all in different-size fancy frames. She must be an only child, because there aren't pictures of anyone else. She's also by herself in every picture, instead of with a parent or friend, which makes her seem a little lonely, even though she's smiling in the photos. I wonder if she had friends at her old school, and feel glad that she already seems to have made so many here.

Micah comes back and grabs my arm. "Come on, slowpoke," he says. He doesn't even notice the photos.

The backyard has an in-ground pool in the middle of it, with a cement walkway all around and big lawn chairs spread out in various places. A bunch of people are already in the pool. When Sam and Sierra see us, they both wave. They're wearing bikinis. I put my hand in front of the little stain on my shirt.

"Cute hair," Sierra says when we walk to the edge of the pool. Instead of a clown nose, her pimple, which is a lot smaller, is now the center of a cute little flower.

"Thanks," I say. "Cute flower."

Sierra smirks. "I got smart and used permanent marker this time so it doesn't turn into a horror flower."

Sam rolls her eyes. "Could you do that to my hair?"

she asks, crossing her arms at the side of the pool to hold herself up.

"My mom did it," I say.

She looks disappointed.

"But I bet she'd do it for you. She loves doing hair."

This is a lie. My mom would probably hate doing Sam's hair. She doesn't have time. And I don't know why I said it.

No. That's a lie, too. I know why I said it. To impress her. To make her like me as much as she likes Micah.

The doorbell rings in the distance, and Sierra's mom disappears again.

"I wonder if that's Jack and Evan," Sam says. She uses her arms to lift herself out of the pool. Her bikini bottoms barely cover her. My parents would probably never let me wear something that skimpy. Not that I'd want to.

She shakes her wet hair when she stands up, spraying water on me and Micah.

"C'mon, Sierra. Get out so we can greet them."

Sierra uses the ladder on the side of the pool. Her bikini is just as skimpy as Sam's. I'm glad I'm still wearing my clothes, and try to think of a way to avoid going into the pool. I am going to look ridiculous next to

them in my little-girl one-piece. Also, I realize I forgot
to bring a towel.

"Hey, guys!" Sam says in her flirty way.

Jack and Evan are already wearing their bathing
suits and no shirts. They each have towels draped over
their shoulders and walk over to us confidently, like
they've practiced their look. I wonder if, when Micah
looks at these two, he feels the same way that I do when
I look at Sam and Sierra: totally inadequate.

They shake hands with Micah and say, "Hey, Rachel,"
to me.

"You look different," Evan says, staring at me.

"It's her hair," Sam butts in. "Isn't it cute?"

"Uh, yeah," Evan says, blushing.

"You guys wanna swim?" Sierra asks. "There's food
over there, too." She gestures toward a picnic table on
the far side of the pool. There's an umbrella over it with
twinkle lights along the rim. The table is crowded with
bowls of snacks.

"How many people are coming?" Micah asks.

"Oh, just practically our whole class," Sam says.

"Sam!" Sierra says. "I told you no more than twenty
people!"

Sam grins. "Don't worry. I'm sure they won't *all*
show up."

Sierra smacks her playfully. "I told Sam to invite people since I don't know anyone," she explains.

"Yeah, this is an 'Everyone Meet the New Girl Party,'" Sam says.

I catch Evan staring at the flower on Sierra's cheek, slowly figuring out what's in the center. He looks a little grossed out.

The doorbell rings again. "And here they all come!" Sierra says. "Oh, man."

"Don't be nervous," Sam says. "I only invited nice people."

"We're not nice," Jack jokes.

Sam elbows him. He grabs her playfully and drags her to the edge of the pool. She fake-screams as he pulls her over the side. Evan runs after them and cannonballs into the water.

Micah smiles at me awkwardly. The two of us look so lame next to everyone else. It's like they all turned into teenagers and we're still kids.

"Are you going in?" he asks.

"I forgot my towel," I say.

"We can share. C'mon."

"Not yet," I say. "I think I'll just hang out here."

I sit on the outstretched lawn chair and he sits next to me protectively. Sierra's mom ushers over a bunch of people from school who wave at us, then strip to their suits and jump in the pool. Pretty soon there are definitely more than twenty people here, and they are all in the pool, splashing and laughing. Micah and I look even more lame, not joining in the fun.

"Well, I'm going in," Micah says, losing patience. "Are you coming or not?"

I wish I'd gone in right away because now I have to take off my clothes and everyone will see my bathing suit before I can hide in the water. I take off my T-shirt and shorts as quickly as possible and hurry to the edge of the pool, but it's so crowded, I can't just jump in. It feels like everyone is looking at me, quietly laughing at my childish bathing suit. No other girl here is wearing a one-piece.

"C'mon in, Rachel," Sam yells, and now everyone really *is* looking at me.

Micah jumps in and swims over to Sierra.

The next thing I know, I feel hands on my waist and I'm falling forward. The people below me all scatter out of the way as I fall into the pool and underwater, a body pushing me under, then pulling me up. Evan.

I gasp and choke.

"Sorry," Evan says. "I slipped as we were going in.

Didn't mean to drag you under! Are you OK?"

I wipe my nose and the water out of my eyes. "I'm fine," I say, reaching with my feet to see if I can stand up.

"Your . . ." he gestures to the back of my head. "It kind of came undone?"

I feel the back of my head, and a braid is hanging loose out of my bun. My cheeks are on fire as I struggle with the barrette and elastics to free my hair, then dunk under again to make it smooth. I look around for Micah so I can give him the evil eye and curse him for making me come to this stupid party, but he's at the other end of the pool, in a circle with Sam and Sierra, not even noticing me.

"So, what homeroom did you get placed in?" Evan asks, treading water in front of me.

"Mr. Jinkerson," I say. "How about you?"

"Yeah, me too!" Evan says. He looks genuinely glad, and for a minute, I think it's because we'll be together. "I heard he's a really great teacher. I have him for English, too," he says.

"So do I!" I say.

"That's great. Maybe we can, like, study together sometimes."

"Oh," I say. "Um. Yeah. Of course."

"Cool."

He lists all the other classes and teachers he has, and it turns out we're going to be in most of the same ones. I know this is flirting, this thing we're doing. He keeps grinning at me in a funny way, and it makes me feel a little pretty. Almost.

"So," he says, after we've been talking for a while, inching farther and farther apart from everyone else. "Do you have a boyfriend?"

"A boyfriend?"

No one has ever asked me this before. Usually the question is "Why haven't you ever had a boyfriend?" Or "Is Micah your boyfriend, or what?" I know we are only going into eighth grade, but by now everyone has had some sort of relationship, even if it only means sending a note that says *I like you. Do you like me?* and then "going out" for a few days but never actually speaking a word to each other.

Down at the far side of the pool, I watch Micah laughing with Sierra and a bunch of girls.

"No boyfriend," I say.

"Oh. I wasn't sure if you and Micah—"

"Just friends."

"Oh."

His cheeks turn a little pink.

The next thing I know, he's leaning forward and I know what he is about to do and that I should stop him. This is not what I was expecting to happen, and definitely not here. Not now. Not out in the open in front of all these people. And definitely not with Evan!

But then I think, *Just try it.* Maybe it will feel good. Maybe it will make my heart feel like a hummingbird. He's cute. He seems nice. Why not?

Only, I know why not.

Micah.

He's at the other end of the pool, though, flirting with Sierra.

I want to try. Part of me *needs* to try.

He leans closer. When our lips touch, he presses forward a bit more. They're cold and wet from the pool water and feel like rubber. They feel gross. Kissing Evan does not make me feel excited. Or whatever you're probably supposed to feel when a nice, cute boy wants to kiss you. If anything, my heart sinks.

I lean back, away from his lips and his sweet face and his hopeful eyes.

"Sorry," I say.

"What for?" he asks.

"I don't really like public displays of affection."

"Oh." He laughs. "PDAs. I hear you. Want to find someplace to go?"

Someone squeals at the other end of the pool. We both turn to see Sam on Jack's shoulders. Sierra is trying to climb onto Micah's so they can play a game of Chicken. Micah sees me watching and gives me a dirty look.

No. Not a dirty look.

A hurt look.

"I think I'm going to go get some food," I say lamely.

"Sounds great!" Evan says, not getting the hint.

He follows me out of the pool, and we both dry off. I use Micah's towel and hope he won't mind. I keep myself wrapped in it to hide my bathing suit. At the snack table, there are all the things I usually love to eat, but now it all seems gross, which is exactly how I feel, and I just want to get out of here.

"I thought you were hungry," Evan says, chomping on a Dorito.

I pick one up and take a bite. The fake cheese flavor hurts my tongue.

Sierra screams as Sam grabs her hands and they topple off Micah's and Jack's shoulders.

I would give anything to be able to walk home right now.

Evan reaches for my hand and holds tight. "C'mon. Let's go around the side of the house."

"I—"

"C'mon," he says again. He smiles in this suggestive way that makes me kind of hate him. Why can't he get the message?

"I don't think so," I say. "Sorry."

"What?"

He looks surprised that I, plain and boring and unpopular Rachel, would turn him down.

"Sorry," I say again.

He drops my hand. "Suit yourself," he says. He tosses his towel onto an empty chair, runs to the end of the pool, and cannonballs the Chicken players. They all scream and laugh. Micah glances over at me, and I try so hard to say I'm sorry with my expression, but he turns and splashes Sam and pretends to be having the best time of his life in this trying-too-hard way that is just sad and embarrassing.

I stand there with my half-eaten Dorito and feel like I'm going to throw up.

On the walk home, Micah walks faster than me and I can barely keep up.

"Would you slow down?" I keep calling to him.

"I'm not walking fast!" he calls back without turning around.

"Micah! Stop!"

He finally slows down, and I run to catch up. I reach for his arm, but he shakes me off.

"What's wrong?" I ask. "Why are you mad at me?"

"You really have to ask me that, Rachel? Seriously?"

"What?"

"Evan? You kiss *Evan*? I thought the reason you didn't want to be more than friends is because you were . . . that maybe you don't like boys. But it turns out you just don't like me! Why would you let me think that?" He makes a mean face that might be disgust, but I'm not sure.

"Let you think what?" I ask.

"You know what." He says the words as if he's repulsed.

My heart begins to throb in a way it's never hurt before. My chest rises and falls as my heart thumps inside, trying to fight its way through, to show Micah how much it hurts. How much it loves him. How scared it is.

"Micah . . ."

He won't look at me, and I don't know what to say, anyway. I know why he's upset, even if it's not really fair.

"I had to try," I finally say.

He starts walking away from me.

"You could have tried with me!" he yells over his shoulder.

"No, I couldn't!" I yell back.

He turns and stomps toward me.

"Really? Why not?"

"Because! It would . . . It would ruin everything!"

"How do you know?" The hurt pulses across his face.

"I just do, OK? I didn't really want to kiss Evan, but he was just . . . there. And I thought if I let him kiss me, I could know for sure that—" The thumping in my chest turns to a horrible ache.

"Know for sure what?" he asks quietly.

"That I wouldn't feel anything. When a boy kissed me. And I was right. We kissed and nothing happened." A tear, then another, escapes down my cheek. "I didn't feel anything."

He looks at me carefully, as if he's trying to figure out what that means.

A sob bumps out of me, and more tears escape down my cheeks.

"What's wrong with me?" I ask.

"Don't be so overdramatic. Nothing's wrong with you. You know what this means."

"What does it mean?"

"What you've always known."

"Don't be mysterious," I say, even though I know exactly what he's implying.

"I'm not going to spell it out for you, Rachel. You're the one who needs to accept it."

"I don't know how."

"Well, what do you want me to do?" he asks.

"Stop being so cold and angry. Stop acting like I have a choice. Say that we'll always be together anyway."

I wipe my cheeks with my hands and sniff, but I can't stop crying.

I want him to hug me, but I know he isn't going to. He's the only person on the planet I can even try to talk to about this stuff, and he's too disappointed to want to help.

I stand there and let my tears continue to slip down my cheeks. He doesn't try to make me feel better. He just stares at me, and I blink back at him.

Finally he rolls his eyes and takes my hand and pulls me along the road like he did when we were little. I let him, but it doesn't feel the same as it did back then. It doesn't feel like he wants my hand in his. Like he wants to take me home to safety. Like he wants to be with me at all.

When I picture myself at the far end of the pool with Evan, and imagine how Micah must have felt watching us, I don't blame him.

As he pulls me along, my hair hanging limply and making my T-shirt wet, I realize I lost my rainbow barrette.

And maybe my best friend.

༄ Chapter Eleven ༈

When we get to my house, Micah finds his bike and leaves without even saying good-bye.

My parents start asking questions the minute I walk in the door.

"How'd it go?"

"Did you have fun?"

"What's Sierra like?"

"Are her parents nice?"

"Why didn't Micah come in with you?"

"What happened to your hair?"

"I'm tired," I tell them. "It was fine." They don't push it when I walk away and start up the stairs.

Ivy is sitting on the top step with George.

"What are you doing?" I ask.

"Waiting."

"Why?"

"I want to know how the party went. What was it like?"

"Not you, too?"

George cranes his head forward for a pat. I rub behind his ears, and he starts to purr.

What I really want is to go hide and not talk to anyone, but I can tell Ivy has been waiting all this time for me to come home and share.

"C'mon," I say. "Let's go to my room."

We sit on my bed, and Ivy gets comfy with George.

"It wasn't a big deal," I say. "It was just like a birthday party but without presents. We swam and ate junk food."

"Did you play Spin the Bottle?"

"What? No."

"I thought that's what you did at middle-school parties."

"Not this one."

"Well, what did you play?"

"It's middle school, Ivy. You don't play anymore."

"Then what did you do all night?"

I see myself stuck at the end of the pool with Evan. I imagine again how we looked to Micah, talking and laughing and then . . .

"Nothing," I say. "It was actually really boring."

"Getting older sucks."

"Don't say *sucks*. It sounds weird coming out of you."

"Whatever. I just don't want to have to stop having fun and stuff."

"Just because you get older doesn't mean you have to stop having fun. And don't say *whatever,* either."

"Well, you never have any fun. All you do is worry about everything."

George pads over to my end of the bed and starts circling. I press him down to make him stop, and he stops purring and looks at me.

"You aren't even nice to the cat!" Ivy says.

"I am, too!" I rub George's ears to make him purr again. "I just don't like it when he circles around forever."

Ivy leans back against the wall and looks up at the paper lantern light in the middle of my ceiling. Micah and I colored it with markers when we were young. We made flowers across the middle in a green field, sea creatures in the ocean all around the bottom, and a black sky with yellow stars at the top. My mom had a fit when she saw what we'd done, but when we turned the light on inside the lantern, it looked really pretty and she forgave us.

"Do you miss being a kid?" Ivy asks.

I look at the chipmunk Micah drew in the green field next to the brown-and-white rabbit I drew. They are sitting under a giant purple flower. I think it's supposed to be a lilac, which doesn't make sense as far as what grows in a field, but of course makes sense given our engagement under the lilac bushes all those years ago.

"Yeah," I say. "All the time."

Ewe and Me stare longingly at their gate the next morning, as if they are both daydreaming about life on the outside. I imagine them escaping and trotting down the road, stopping at each field they come across to graze and decide if this is the place where they should stay awhile. Then I start to imagine what would happen if *all* the animals stepped outside their pens. Would they want to leave? Or would they just stand and look bewildered? Maybe they'd wander from pen to pen to see if they preferred someplace else. The way they stare at one another all day, I'm sure they're sizing up the other areas, wondering if they have it better or worse than their neighbors. Maybe they're wondering if the grass really is greener on the other side of the fence. Mr. Townsend says they need to get to know one another before they can all share the same pasture with Ben and

Gil. Sometimes I wonder where he gets his information and whether it's accurate. But I hope I get to see them when they all get to run free together.

I lug Lucy's feed over to her pen and set it down just outside the fence by the hook. I watch her carefully before attempting to climb up and latch the bucket on her side. She's sunning herself in a muddy area at the far corner of her pen. A tiny breeze drifts over her and sends her stench directly into my face. It's as if she made it happen, and I bet she smiles inside when the smell hits me. It sure is hard to love the hell out of this pig.

"Morning, Lucy," I say.

She opens one little beady eye and closes it again. She flicks her tail and grunts, then rolls over so her back is to me. But she's not fooling me. Her hooves quiver, ready to jump into action and charge the minute I put one foot on the fence. I lift the bucket carefully, not taking my eyes off her. She doesn't move. I take one step toward the fence, then another. In slow motion, I put one foot on the lower rail. An ear twitches, but I can't tell if it's from the breeze or from her piggy senses when she hears the sound of my foot touching the wood. I grab the upper rail and slowly hoist myself up. The bucket is heavy to lift with one hand. I pull the bucket over as quietly as possible, but just as I start to lower it to the other side, Lucy jumps to her feet. I don't know how she can move so fast for such a big pig. It's as if her whole loaf of a body just pops up in the air and flips, like a giant piece of toast popping out of a toaster.

She charges.

I scramble with the bucket handle, trying to get it in the metal latch as she cannonballs toward me like a pink tank.

"Ohhhhh, nooooo, youuuuuu, donnnnnnnt," I mutter, frantically trying to get the handle in the latch. It snaps in place, Lucy body-slams the fence, and I fall backward into the dirt. The food in the bucket spills all over her snout, and she grunts in a satisfied way, shaking her head proudly.

"Dumb pig," I say.

She twitches her tail and ignores me, scarfing down her breakfast without a care. But I wonder. I wonder what it is about me, about getting this food, that makes her slam her body against the fence every time. Does she like getting the feed all over her face and on the ground? Or does she like this one moment of power she has, when she can show she can do more than wallow in mud and sunbathe and get fat enough so that someday . . . ? Just thinking about her fate makes me feel sorry for her again. Sorry for all the animals out there whose only purpose is to get fat so someone can eat them. I step back up onto the fence and she lifts her head, confused. This is not part of our routine.

"Hey, girl," I say.

She grunts.

"Why do you like bashing me off the fence, anyway?"

She crams her nose back into the feed bucket and finishes quietly. When she's done, she looks up at me again. Her tiny dark eyes are surrounded by light-colored lashes, the same color as her pink hair. Her snout still has food on it, and she licks it, not taking her eyes off me.

Slowly I reach my hand out. She sniffs the air in front of it suspiciously.

"I won't hurt you," I say, reaching farther. "Do you want a pat?"

She shifts her weight from foot to foot and flicks her tail, still sniffing. Her eyes narrow, as if she was expecting some food in my hand. What would happen if I set her free? Where would she go?

"Do you want out of here?" I ask her.

She opens her mouth and shows me her sharp teeth. I imagine them clamping over my fingers, and I pull my hand away. She turns and trots back to her corner of the pen and circles around before settling herself down, just like George does.

"Well, suit yourself," I tell her. I climb off the fence and find Ferdinand.

He seems extra-excited to see me and slurps up his formula, then head-butts my thigh to tell me he wants to play. I walk him around the yard to visit all the other animals. Ewe and Me run around their pen excitedly as if they want me to let him in to play.

Ferdinand pokes his nose through the fence, and the sheep both touch noses with him, then run away again. It makes me want to put them all in the pasture now, so they won't be lonely, but I'd probably get in trouble. I certainly wouldn't trust Lucy with them. I bet she'd try to body-slam them all into the fence. Unless I'm the only one she hates.

After we visit the horses, I put Ferdinand back in his pen. He looks so sad that I take him out and walk him around again. Just as I'm putting him back a second time, I hear a car door shut in the distance. I start to walk back up toward the house and find the Townsends in the driveway, their two little dogs yipping in circles.

"Hi, Rachel!" Mr. Townsend calls. When the dogs see me, they come running, barking like mad.

"Thought we'd come back early to see how your first week went. Looks like you took a tumble."

I brush the dried-up dirt from my shorts while the dogs try to jump on me. "Lucy," I say. "She likes to try to knock me off the fence when I feed her."

Mrs. Townsend makes a face, but Mr. Townsend laughs and pats me on the back reassuringly. "That means she likes you," he says. "She doesn't even pay attention to me, the evil thing. Just like my sister-in-law."

"Bev!" Mrs. Townsend says.

"You know it's true."

"How's everyone else doing, Rachel?" Mrs. Townsend asks.

"Fine," I say. "Ferdinand seems a little lonely, though."

"Aww, poor little guy," Mr. Townsend says. "We'll go say hi to him. He loves the dogs."

I find this hard to believe.

"Have you got any weekend plans?" he asks me.

"Not really."

"Well, you can take the afternoon shift off since we came back early. I'll drop a check in your mailbox."

"Oh, OK," I say. "Thanks."

"Have a good weekend!" They leave me in the

driveway. Mr. Townsend whistles as they go. It puts me in a happy mood, until I realize I'm out two hours of pay.

Back at home, the house is quiet. My parents are at work, and Ivy is watching cartoons from the DVD discards my mom brought home from the library. We used to have cable, but my parents stopped paying, so now all we can watch are old DVDs. When my mom still worked for the school, we could go online and stream shows and do our homework on the laptop they let her bring home, but she had to give it back when she lost her job.

"Hey," I say. "Did you eat breakfast yet?"

She lifts up a cereal bowl without answering.

"You're not supposed to eat on the couch," I say.

"It's just cereal. I'm not getting crumbs anywhere."

"You could spill."

"I'm not a baby."

I leave her and search for food in the kitchen. The cupboard we keep the cereal in is empty. "Did you eat the last of the cereal?" I yell.

"Sorry!"

Usually there's at least *something* in the cupboard, like cornflakes at the very least.

I check the bread box for English muffins, but there's just a bag of bread with only the heels left.

In the fridge, I find an orange that's a little bit squishy but seems OK. I can't remember the last time my parents let us get so low on food. But I can't remember the last time they've been so worried about money, either.

I cut the orange in quarters and put them on a plate, then join Ivy in front of the TV.

"You're not supposed to eat in here," she says, mocking my voice.

"Shut up," I say.

George wanders in and jumps up on the couch to sit between us.

Ivy pops in a *SpongeBob* DVD.

"Can I have an orange wedge?" Ivy asks.

"Seriously? This is all I have for breakfast."

"I'm hungry," she whines.

I hand her a wedge.

"I hope Mom and Dad go shopping soon," she says. "We're running out of everything."

I think of the two hours of pay I'm losing today and how many boxes of cereal it could buy.

"Me too," I say. The orange juice in my belly feels like acid burning my insides.

"Are we going to the beach?"

"I doubt it," I say.

"How come? It's sunny!"

I really don't feel like talking about Micah and our fight, so I just tell her I think Micah is busy today. She gives me a funny look like she knows I'm not telling the truth, but she doesn't ask me to explain. Instead, she slurps the milk out of her cereal bowl and puts it on the floor. George jumps down and licks it.

"Gross," I say.

Ivy leans back on the couch and snuggles as the theme song to *SpongeBob* finally starts.

"You've seen this a million times," I say. "Haven't you outgrown it yet? We could go to the library and check out some new movies."

"No. It's comforting," she tells me.

"You're such a weirdo."

She sinks lower into the couch and, just to annoy me, sings along to the opening music as loud as she can.

In my room, I find my phone and check for messages. Zero. Usually by late morning, I have at least ten from Micah telling me to wake up, sending me funny cat GIFs, or *something*. But today, nothing. I guess it won't be long before we can't afford to buy more minutes for my phone anyway, so it doesn't matter. I flop on my bed and watch out the window. Every so often, the breeze picks up and sends the smell of summer across the bed. I roll over and watch my lantern sway when the breeze comes through the window. I think about how, whenever Micah and I worked on something like the lantern, we'd talk for hours about everything under the sun. About what we wanted to be when we grew up. About where we would live. About how many kids we'd have. And what kind of pets. I never felt uncomfortable around Micah. We never ran out of things to talk about, or felt like we had to fill the silence when we just didn't want to talk for a while. We have always been perfect friends. Always, except for when he wanted to be more than that.

I try to imagine what it would have been like to kiss him instead of Evan last night.

But I don't want to kiss him.

Hug him, yes. Hold his hand, yes. Lie next to him and look up at the sky and daydream, yes. But not kiss. I try to think of any boy I might like to kiss, and there isn't one. There never has been, as long as I can remember. Not since that time under the lilac bushes. But back then, it wasn't the kissing that made my heart flutter. It was the excitement of doing something I'd never done. And realizing how much I loved Micah. Back then, I didn't know the difference between loving a friend and loving someone for any other reason.

In health class last year, we did a unit on sexual health, and we learned all about sex and gender and reproduction. Our teacher, Ms. Lane, said a lot of people know from an early age which sex they're attracted to, but some aren't sure. And some like both. When she said the part about how some people know from an early age, you could tell everyone kind of gazed at Will and Tony. They are the first boy-boy couple to be open about it in our grade. Will raised his hand and said boldly, "That's me! I've always known I was gay." A few people laughed, and Tony blushed and said quietly, "Me too."

"Perfect example," Ms. Lane said, looking a little awkward.

"Well, I've always known I'm straight as a door!" Cole Jenkins said.

"Heterosexual," Ms. Lane corrected.

Cole rolled his eyes.

After that, Ms. Lane gave us this big list of names for how people identify themselves, and it was really confusing. I think by the end of class, no one really knew what to make of any of it or where we fit. Even Cole Jenkins looked confused.

"You can be *fluid*," Ms. Lane had said. She made it

sound complicated and simple at the same time. The truth is, she can say all that stuff, and be really understanding, but I don't know if in the real world people are all that open-minded. Even at school, people can be weird about things. It's one thing for Ms. Lane to tell us that her classroom is a safe space, but people still gossip and it doesn't always feel like no one's judging. And besides, there's a lot more to the school than Ms. Lane's classroom.

People want to know if you are straight or something else. But the *something else* implies that it's something other than "normal." Will and Tony are lucky no one gives them a hard time. In some places, they would probably get bullied or beat up. And that scares me, too.

I hate the word *straight*.

I bet it makes everyone else feel crooked. Or slanted. Or not perfect.

George wanders into my room and meows. I drop my hand over the side of the bed, and he comes over and rubs his head under my fingers. I scratch behind his ears, and he starts to purr. I pat the blanket near my chest, and he jumps up. He walks over to sniff my face and touch his cold wet nose to mine, then circles a few times before plopping down next to my head. He continues to purr reassuringly, as if he knows I need a friend.

I twist Micah's friendship bracelet on my wrist and watch my phone, hoping maybe my friend, who only yesterday promised we'd be together forever, will decide to check in after all. But it never buzzes. After a while, Ivy comes in to tell me she's bored, so we go outside. I lift her up on Rainbow, and I sit on my mom's old lawn chair and read *Charlotte's Web*.

"For inspiration," Ivy said when she chose the book.

"Inspiration for what?" I asked.

"On how to save Lucy."

༄ Chapter Twelve ༄

When we go back inside, I check my phone for texts. There's one from an unknown number: *Hey, Rachel! It's Sierra. Come to the beach later!*

I bet Sam gave her my number, or maybe Micah! I add her name to my contacts. Like a real friend. Maybe she is one! Then I text Micah.

Me: *Are you going to the beach?*

Micah:

Me: *I think we should go.*

Micah:

Read

Me: *I know you're there. Reply!*

Micah:

Read

I scroll through GIFs and find a sad-looking kitten to send him.

Me: [*sad kitten*]

Micah:

Read

I wait and wait, but he doesn't answer.

Me: *You're not being very fair.*

I glance around the room, trying to remember if I hung up my wet bathing suit after the party or not. I see it on the floor, underneath my stupid stained T-shirt. The bird on the sleeve is wrinkled and looks like it has a broken wing. I'm sure everyone else at the beach will have different bathing suits on from what they wore last night. My suit is still a little damp, so I run downstairs and throw it in the dryer, even though we're supposed to use the clothesline outside in the summer.

"Hey!" Ivy says, coming up behind me. "You're not supposed to use that."

"It's an emergency."

"Why?"

"Because Sierra invited me to the beach and my suit is kind of gross."

"Can I come?"

"No."

"But I don't want to stay home alone! You're supposed to stay with me."

"Mom and Dad will be home in a few hours."

"That's too long!"

"Well, little kids aren't invited. You know how to take care of yourself. You can just watch *SpongeBob* all afternoon."

"I'm tired of *SpongeBob*."

"I thought he was comforting."

She pouts.

"Don't be a baby."

"Micah won't care if I go."

"Micah won't be there."

"Why not?"

"How should I know?" I know I'm being a jerk, but I can't seem to stop myself.

Ivy stands there looking let down in this pitiful way.

"Ivy, please just let me go alone this one time." I try to soften my voice, but I still feel bad.

"Why can't I go? I won't even sit near you."

"Because it's the lake, and I'd be responsible for you not drowning."

"That's what the lifeguard is for!"

She looks like she might cry. If Micah could see this scene, he would be so disappointed in me. I can just feel him judging me.

Is it really such a big deal to bring her along? What's the worst that could happen? She could embarrass me.

She could tell everyone stories about me. But . . . she wouldn't do that.

"Fine," I finally say. "You can come. But you owe me a big favor. Huge."

She jumps up and down and wraps her arms around my waist. She smells a little funky.

"When was the last time you took a bath?" I ask.

"It's summer. I don't need a bath. I just go to the lake!"

"There's this thing called soap. And another called shampoo."

"Bad for the environment."

"But good for not stinking."

She shrugs. "I don't care if I stink!"

"Obviously."

She beams at me even though I'm insulting her.

"Go get your beach stuff and we'll pack some snacks to bring with us, OK?"

"Yes!"

She races down the hall and stomps up the stairs as she chants, "We! Are! Going! To! The! Beach!"

I wish small stuff like this could make me as happy as that. It's depressing how, as I get older, things that make me happy seem much harder to get. Like my parents being able to pay the bills. Or me finding a job that would pay enough that I could really help. Or being able to talk with my best friend about how confused I am without having him stop speaking to me.

I wait twenty minutes, then check to see if my suit is dry. Good enough. I get dressed and check my phone again, but there are no new messages from Micah.

I send him a simple message: *Leaving for the beach now. Hope to see you there. Sorry about the party.*

I don't wait to see if he reads it. I shove my phone in my back pocket and yell to Ivy to come on down and help me find some food to bring.

We scrounge around in the kitchen, but there's really nothing to eat other than pasta and mac and cheese in a box. There's one sleeve of Saltines and an almost-empty jar of peanut butter, so we scrape as much out as we can and make "essence of peanut butter" crackers.

"We should call Mom and tell her there isn't any food in the house," Ivy says grumpily.

"I'm sure she knows," I say. "Let's not bother her. I'm supposed to get paid today. Maybe when we get home from the beach, my check will be in the mailbox and we can ride bikes to town and get some treats."

"Really?"

I think about how much it would cost to get some

more crackers and squeeze cheese, Ivy's favorite. I should still have money left after that to help pay for a bill or two.

"Yup," I say. "And if you are a really good sister and don't embarrass me at the beach, I'll even let you get an ice-cream sandwich."

"Me? Embarrass you?" She gives me a mischievous look and waddles toward the front door.

"What are you doing?" I ask.

"Getting all my weirdness out of my system before we get to the beach!"

She lets out a toot.

"Why are you so gross?" I ask.

She just giggles and shakes her bum.

❧ Chapter Thirteen ❧

There are so many bikes locked on the bike rack that we have trouble finding a place for ours. I look for Micah's bike but don't see it.

"I could leave mine unlocked and no one would take it," Ivy says, struggling with her rusty bike lock.

"Just to be safe," I tell her.

The beach is a patchwork of towels. We wind our way along the shore, toward the far end, which used to be Micah's and my spot but now seems to be taken over by the incoming eighth grade. I can't believe how many people are here. I wonder what it is about Sierra that makes people flock to her, flower pimple and all. She waves when she sees us and jumps up from her towel to run over.

Her pimple is almost gone, so she didn't bother to

draw anything on it today. She has a new bikini on, too. It's purple with red hearts.

"Hi, guys," she says. "Where's Micah?"

Ivy tilts her head up at me.

"He didn't return my text," I say.

"Hmm. Well, maybe he'll show up later. Wanna swim?"

"Yes!" Ivy says.

Sierra smiles at her. "I'll race you to the line!"

Ivy drops her towel and bike helmet at my feet and runs into the water. They turn and splash me, then dive under as soon as they get out deep enough. I pick up Ivy's towel and walk to where the rest of the group has spread out their stuff. Evan is there, but he doesn't say hello, so I don't, either.

"Hey, Rachel!" Sam says. She moves to one side of her towel and pats it for me to sit next to her. She has a different bathing suit on from the party, too. I keep my T-shirt and shorts on but kick my flip-flops off in the sand.

"You need a pedicure," Sam says.

I blush and dig my toes in the sand.

"Oh! I mean, not because your toes are ugly, you just . . . you should put some polish on them! Sierra has some really cute decals she'd share. Look!" She shows me her toes, which are painted bright orange. There are little sun decals on her two big toes.

"Fun," I say lamely.

"Hey, Rachel, how's your summer going so far?" It's Cybil Jackson. We've never been good friends, but she seems nice.

"Oh, hi. It's OK. How's yours?"

When she talks to me, she looks me right in the eye. It makes me feel funny.

"I have to work for my dad at the pharmacy, which stinks. But other than that it's OK." She wiggles her toes in the sand. I notice she doesn't have any nail polish on, either. She catches me looking. "I hate nail polish," she whispers just to me.

"You guys want to go in the water?" Sam asks.

"Definitely," Cybil says.

They both pop up and walk toward the shoreline. Evan, Will, Tony, and a bunch of other boys join them. Will and Tony hold hands when they race into the water. I think they must be the longest-dating couple in our grade.

"You coming, Rach?" Sam asks.

"Be right there," I say.

I wait until they're all far out near the line before I slowly take off my T-shirt and shorts and run in as quickly as possible before anyone can see that I'm wearing the same lame bathing suit from the party.

Sierra and Ivy swim over to me and splash until I dip my head under. We play Clueless for a while, then Ivy says she's hungry, so I tell her to go get our crackers out of the backpack.

"Your little sister is so cute," Sierra says.

Cybil swims over to join us. "She's gotten so much older! Remember in kindergarten when she was a baby and your dad brought her in every day for that unit on infant development? That was so fun."

"I forgot all about that!" I say.

"The other kindergarten class was so jealous," Sam says, swimming around our circle.

Cybil keeps smiling at me, like she just discovered who I was or something. It's kind of weird.

"But she would only let you hold her. If anyone else tried to, she'd start screaming bloody murder," Cybil says.

"I can't believe you remember that," I tell her.

Cybil nods. "And Mrs. Crowley wanted Ivy to be an honorary member of kindergarten."

The memories all come to me now: our kindergarten class sitting in a circle on the floor, Ivy lying in a swaddled bundle in the center, cooing and trying to wriggle free. We weighed her once a week and kept track of each milestone, like sucking her thumb and smiling and a bunch of other stuff I don't really remember.

"People go nuts around babies," Sam says, swimming into the center of our circle.

"Well, they're pretty adorable," Sierra says, twirling herself around and around. "Until you have to change their diaper."

We all giggle.

"What's so funny?" Evan asks as he, Jack, and the others swim over to join us.

"Diapers," Sam says.

"Gross," Evan says. He dives underwater, and a few seconds later Sam screeches. Then someone grabs my foot, and instead of screeching, I kick reflexively. Hard.

Jack bobs up out of the water. "Ow!" he says, glaring at me.

"Sorry!" I say. "You scared me."

He looks at me like I'm a freak.

"That's what you get for being a creeper," Sam tells him.

He rolls his eyes and swims over to her. "You know you like it."

"Gross," Cybil says.

"I'm going to go check on Ivy." I swim away from them and head to shore. Ivy is stuffing her face and getting crumbs all over my towel.

"Hey! Why aren't you sitting on your own towel? Get off!"

"Yours was nice and warm. I forgot to spread mine out."

"Seriously? Get off now."

She stands up and gets sand all over the place. My towel is soaked.

"Sorry," she says. "You can have mine."

"Never mind. I just need to dry off."

She finds her towel and wraps it around her like a dress while holding the empty bag of crackers in her mouth.

"Glad I'm not hungry," I say. "Thanks for leaving me some."

"I have some food to share," a voice says behind me.

It's Cybil. I didn't realize she'd followed me out of the water.

I blush, realizing I sounded like a jerk just now, being mean to Ivy.

"What do you have?" Ivy asks.

"Same as you, actually," Cybil says.

"Essence of peanut butter? Shoot."

"Essence?" Cybil asks.

"The jar was almost empty, so we had to make do," I explain.

"I'm pretty sure my crackers have more than essence." She walks over to her backpack to rummage for snacks. She's wearing a two-piece like everybody else. I quickly wrap my towel around myself.

Cybil straightens and shakes a sandwich bag with peanut butter crackers in it. "Want some? Looks like plenty of peanut butter in there."

"Sure."

We sit side by side on her towel, me still wrapped in mine. Ivy stretches out on her own towel, tummy down, and closes her eyes.

Cybil and I eat quietly and watch the group play Chicken out in the water.

"I never really liked that game," Cybil says. "It's so sexist."

"Yeah," I say, not really knowing why it's sexist. Maybe because it's always the girls climbing on the boys' shoulders and not the other way around.

Each time we pass the sandwich bag back and forth, our fingers touch. When our eyes meet, Cybil smiles at me the way Evan did that night at the pool, when we first started talking, before we kissed. At least that's how it feels. I look over at Ivy to see if she's watching, but her eyes are closed and there's a little drool coming out of her mouth.

"She fell asleep!" I whisper.

Cybil giggles. "She was a lot cuter when she was a baby."

"Tell me about it."

She leans closer to me so our arms touch. She's warm. A funny feeling spreads down my arm. My heart starts to beat faster, and I think about that time Micah and I hid under the lilac bush, when it felt like there were hummingbirds in my chest. I take a deep breath and will the feeling to go away, and just like that, I see a pair of familiar bare feet in front of ours.

"Hi," Micah says. "Sorry I ignored your texts."

I put my finger to my lips and gesture to Ivy, who's still sleeping and drooling.

"Hi, Cybil," Micah whispers.

"Hey," she says.

Micah drops his backpack next to us. He doesn't look at me.

"Why aren't you guys swimming?" he asks.

"We don't approve of Chicken," Cybil says.

"Uh, why?"

"It's dumb?"

"Oh."

Micah does not seem very impressed with Cybil, and I think the feeling is mutual. He pulls his T-shirt over his head and drops it on top of his bag. "Well, suit yourselves," he says, then turns and runs into the water, diving under and disappearing toward the chickens.

"You guys still best friends?" Cybil asks quietly.

I look over at Ivy again to make sure she isn't listening. "I . . . think so. We kind of got in a fight last night after the party."

"Yeah, I heard. I'm starting to feel glad I couldn't go. Sounds awkward."

"You heard? Who told you? What did they say?"

"Oh, don't worry. It was just Sam being gossipy. She said you made out with Evan and Micah got jealous."

"Oh, my gosh. I did not make out with Evan!" I say too loudly.

Ivy stirs but seems to stay asleep.

"We kissed," I say. "It's different. And I didn't even really want to."

"Why not?"

We watch him out in the water, Sierra wriggling on top of his shoulders.

"He's a chicken," I say.

Cybil giggles.

"I don't mean that in a mean way," I say. "It's just . . ."

"He's not your type."

"Right."

"So, who is your type?"

I watch Micah kind of taking part and kind of not. He looks like he really wants to be in the group but doesn't know how to mix in. It's how I've always felt, too, and probably why we've been best friends forever. I don't know what it is about us that makes us feel a bit like outsiders. When we were younger, we always liked to play the same things in the same way. We made up elaborate stories we'd act out in the yard or in the woods that my other friends never seemed interested in. We made up special rules for riding our bikes over obstacle courses in the driveway that no one else wanted to follow. When we drew, we made a single picture that we created together, instead of two separate ones. We've been this way as far back as I can remember. So I guess *Micah* is my type. Only . . . he's not.

"I'm not sure," I say lamely.

Cybil doesn't answer for a while. She seems to be studying each person out in the water, searching. Then she turns to look at me again. My cheeks burn like crazy.

"I made you blush," Cybil says. "Sorry."

"No, it's OK."

"I guess I don't really believe in types. It was a dumb question. Sorry. Boy, did I make this awkward."

I laugh a little, not really sure what she means by *this*.

"What do you think? Do you think people just like one type, or do you believe in 'fluidity,' like Ms. Lane taught us last year?"

"Do you mean when a person can like boys but then like girls, or . . . change?" I feel so stupid for not really grasping the concept yet, even after that class.

"Close enough," Cybil says. "Yeah."

"I guess I never thought about it. I mean, well, that's not true. I just didn't think about it with that label."

"Oh. Yeah. You're not a labels person. Me either. I mean they're always changing anyway, right?"

I think about the confusing list Ms. Lane gave us. "Right!" I say. It's such a relief to be able to talk to someone other than Micah about this.

"Well, I'll tell you how I feel," Cybil says, leaning closer to me. "I think I'm attracted to *people*, not their gender. So if I like you, for example, it's not because you're a girl, but just because I like who you are. And sometimes that might mean that I just want to be your friend, and sometimes that might mean that I want to be more than friends. I can't control who I'm attracted to in a more-than-friends way."

Her arm is pressing against mine now. It feels nice.

"I feel like I'm too young to know who I'm attracted to," I say. "Most of the time, anyway."

"But you're not attracted to Micah," she says. "And not Evan."

"No," I say. "Not either of them. I love Micah, but he's only a friend. And I think Evan is nice, sort of, but I'm not really interested in him beyond talking about school and stuff. We really don't have anything else in common."

"Who *have* you had a crush on?"

"I—" I pause for a minute, realizing I don't think I've ever had a crush on someone. How is that even possible? "This is going to sound crazy, but I've never had one," I say.

"Whoa, seriously? I've had a million!"

"Like who?" I ask, trying to shift the focus away from me.

"Oh, Cole Jenkins, Evan, Tony, Sam . . ."

"Who's Sam?" I ask. "Is he from a different school?"

"No, silly. Our Sam." She points to the water, where Sam is about to fall off Jack's shoulders.

I don't know if I'm more surprised that she had a crush on a girl or that she had a crush on Sam, but I try to be nonchalant about it.

"Our Sam? But she's—" I pause. "A chicken!"

Cybil cracks up. I laugh, too, which wakes Ivy.

She sits up and rubs her eyes, and that's when I realize we forgot to put sunblock on her. How could we do that after what happened to me? But she doesn't seem too burned. "What time is it?" she asks. "Why'd you let me fall asleep?"

"Don't worry—you haven't been asleep that long."

She wipes the dried drool off the side of her mouth.

"I'm hungry," she says.

"You shouldn't be—you ate all of our food."

She pouts.

"You're the one who wanted to come. You could've stayed home and waited for Mom and Dad to get back with groceries."

"I'm going back in the water," she says, all gloomy-faced.

"Good. You can keep Micah company."

"Micah's here?" she asks. She jumps to her feet. "Micah!" she yells, waving crazily. She runs into the water and high-fives Micah when she reaches him.

"Your sister is so funny," Cybil says.

"Yeah," I say. "Except when she's not."

Cybil laughs.

"Anyway, we were talking about Sam," I tell her, feeling a little uncomfortable and a little brave at the same time.

"Oh, well, that was a long time ago. I just liked how outgoing she was and stuff. Now I have a new crush developing."

"Really? Who is it?"

"I'm not ready to say yet. It's still too new."

"Oh."

We sit side by side like that, quietly, the way Micah and I sometimes do. It doesn't feel uncomfortable. Not really. But I can't stop wondering who her crush is on, and if it could be me. I wonder if that's what she's thinking about right now, too, as we watch the chickens tire one another out. It makes me think of the Townsends' chickens, and of poor little Bashful, who always seems left out and forgotten. That's me, I realize, whenever I'm with this group and Micah joins in and forgets about me. Until now. Now maybe I have Cybil, who is willing to watch with me from the sidelines. Not excluded, not really, but not quite fitting in, either.

⌒Chapter Fourteen⌒

Pretty soon, it gets too hot to stay on our towels, so we reluctantly join the crew in the water, but of course just as we do, they all decide they're too cold and need to warm up in the sun. Cybil and I tread in the deep area, letting our hot skin cool in the water. Micah goes off with the group instead of joining us. Even Ivy follows them, though I'm sure she'd prefer to stay in the water. She's probably hoping Micah brought some food.

Cybil tells me about working at the pharmacy, babysitting, and a dog-walking job, and I tell her about the Townsends' animals. I describe trying to feed Lucy and walk Ferdinand, and she describes this baby named Ted who will only take his pacifier out of his mouth when it's time to eat and how he turns purple from screaming if you try to take it out any other time. It's funny how I've known Cybil since kindergarten but we never became good friends. I mean funny in a sad way, because she's really nice and I bet we could have been close. Maybe we can be now.

When we get cold, we join the rest of the group, who are all sunbathing and gossiping about various teachers we'll have next year. Ivy is lying down next to Micah, but she doesn't look very happy and I realize it's the look she gets before she throws up.

I poke her toe with my foot. "You OK?"

She shakes her head.

"Want to go home?"

She nods.

"C'mon, then."

I gather up our stuff, and everyone but Micah says a friendly good-bye to us. At least he tells Ivy he hopes she feels better.

We bike home slowly, me following Ivy so I can keep an eye on her because she seems a bit wobbly. As soon as we're in the driveway, she jumps off her bike and runs inside and starts throwing up in the downstairs bathroom. She's still wearing her bike helmet. My dad is usually the one who has throw-up duty, but my parents aren't home from work yet.

I go into the bathroom and rub her back. The smell of puke makes me gag.

"I feel so awful," Ivy says just before she hurls again. "Boy, I didn't chew very well. There are whole Skittles in there."

"Gross!"

"Look!"

"Ivy, seriously, you're going to make me throw up, too. How much junk did you eat?"

She takes a deep breath and hurls another loud, sloppy gush into the toilet.

"I lost track. Everyone put their stuff in the middle of Sam's towel to share, and I was so hungry I ate most of it. They thought it was funny."

"Micah didn't stop you? He knows better than to let you do that."

"He was too busy flirting with Sierra."

"Really?"

"Mm-hm." She leans back on her heels and wipes her mouth with her hand. "I think I'm done."

She reaches forward to flush and watches her half-digested treats swirl down the drain.

"I feel dizzy."

"Just sit here for a minute." I get her toothbrush

from upstairs and bring her some water in her favorite tiger cup.

"I'm too big for that."

"Since when?"

She shrugs.

"Just take a sip."

"Ew, it tastes weird."

"Water always tastes weird after you puke."

"How come?"

"I have no idea. Brush your teeth and you'll feel better and the water won't taste gross."

I help her up, and she brushes her teeth.

"Turn around and let me get that helmet off you," I say.

"I can do it," Ivy says, reaching to unhook the strap. Sometimes she seems like such a tiny kid, and other times, I can see that soon she won't be.

"C'mon, I'll set you up on the couch and you can watch *SpongeBob*," I say.

"I've outgrown it, remember?"

"Whatever." I find her pillow and a blanket and her tiger cup. The pillow is this old ratty thing my grandmother made as a housewarming gift when my parents moved here. It used to be white, but now it's more "grime," with soft red letters embroidered on it that say *Home Is Where the Heart Is*. When Ivy was a baby, she used to rub the letters with her fingers to help her fall asleep. Now, it's "her" pillow whenever we sit on the couch. It's also kind of disgusting, so no one else wants to touch it anyway.

We decide to change things up and put in an old *Scooby-Doo* DVD.

"Are you and Micah going to make up?" Ivy asks me. "Or are you dumping him for that Cybil girl."

"What? I'm not—sheesh, Ivy. Micah's the one not talking to me. I've tried. And I can be friends with more than one person."

"Unless you're more than friends." She pokes me with her foot from under the blanket.

I blush. "What are you talking about?"

She giggles. "That's what Sam was saying about you two. That you looked like you were in love."

"What the heck? They were gossiping about us?"

"They weren't being mean. Micah didn't seem too happy about it, though. He said it was none of their business."

"He did?"

"Yeah. He still really loves you, even if you aren't friends anymore."

"We're still friends. We're just in a fight. And Cybil and I are *not* a couple."

"Why not?"

"Because we aren't! We hardly even know each other. And—"

"And what?"

I want to say, *She's a girl.* But I don't. Because that shouldn't matter. And I want to teach Ivy that. "And I don't know," I say. "But we're not a couple. We were just talking and getting to know each other. That's what new friends do."

"You don't have to get all worked up," Ivy says, mimicking the way Micah would say it. She takes a sip from her cup, which makes her look like a big kid and a baby at the same time.

I laugh.

"What's so funny?"

"Nothing, you dodo. You're just silly."

"Well, I hope you and Micah make up soon. It's no fun when you aren't together."

"I'll try. Promise."

We spend the rest of the afternoon watching *Scooby-Doo* episodes we've already seen a hundred times. Every so often, I check my phone to see if Micah texted to check on Ivy, but he never does. I think about how Ivy said Micah still loves me, even if we aren't friends. The thought makes me feel so empty inside. Empty, and angry, too. Whatever happened to together forever? Did he just mean, as long as I didn't become friends with anyone else? Or . . . more than friends?

I snuggle closer to Ivy, even though it's hot and she smells funny. She slides the pillow closer to me so we can both touch the soft red letters. Instead, I put my hand on hers and squeeze.

"I love you, Rach," she says, looking up at me.

"I love you, too," I say. "Even if you have a little puke on your cheek."

She smiles mischievously and rubs her cheek on my arm.

ᴄChapter Fifteenᴐ

When my parents get home, they have just one bag of groceries instead of the usual four or five. Ivy starts to ask where the rest of the food is, but I nudge her and she shuts up fast.

"Don't you need to be doing evening chores across the street?" my mom asks as my dad silently puts the groceries away.

"The Townsends came home early and gave me the afternoon off."

"Oh."

"That reminds me, he said my paycheck would be in the mailbox!" I run outside and down the driveway, but when I check, the mailbox is empty except for some junk mail and more bills.

"Well?" Ivy asks when I come back inside. "How much did you get?"

"It wasn't there," I say. "I'll check again later."

"What should we make for dinner?" my dad asks. "We have pasta, pasta, or pasta."

"Pasta!" Ivy yells.

"Rachel, can you go pick some basil in the garden?" my mom asks.

"I'll help!" Ivy says.

Ivy and I go out to the garden together. Most of the vegetables aren't ready to pick yet since it's only late June, but my dad started the basil plants inside, so they've already got nice big leaves. I show Ivy how to pinch them off and leave the stems just so, in order to let new growth keep coming. Once we fill the small bowl my mom gave us, we walk up and down the rest of the rows and I tell Ivy what vegetables will come up soon. She knows most of them without me having to tell her, which is impressive.

"But can you tell the difference between the zucchini and the cucumber vines?" I ask.

She studies both and then points to the plant with the bigger leaves and says, "Zucchini!" But I realize she cheated by looking at the small stone my dad painted a Z on and placed in front of the row.

"Nice try," I say.

She smirks.

Before we go back in, we stop to give Rainbow some love. I give Ivy a leg up and let her ride bareback while I lead Rainbow around the yard. It's funny how you get to know where you live so well. I know where every big rock is, every dip in the land, and every tree that's worth trying to climb. When we were little, Micah and I would make entire villages in the cracks of the stone wall for the old Fisher-Price Little People figures that had been my mom's when she was a kid. We'd divide up sections of the wall so we could make our own "apartments" for our people families, and then have them come and visit each other when we were all done. We made tables and chairs from smaller rocks, and beds out of sticks and grass. Ivy was just a baby then, and she'd crawl over to us and try to play. Sometimes she'd ruin all of our hard work, but it was never a big deal because most of the fun came from building. We'd pretend "Hurricane Ivy" had hit and now our people had to rebuild, bigger, better, and stronger.

Rainbow nudges my thighs with his nose and gets slobber on me.

"No carrots in the garden yet, buddy," I say. I bend down and pick some grass for him, and he gently gums it up into his mouth.

"Rachel! Where's that basil?" my dad calls through the kitchen window.

"Coming!"

Ivy helps me put Rainbow in his stall and fill his water and give him some hay. We hug him good night and start back toward the house.

"Rainbow needs his own mini fridge," Ivy says.

"Nah, that's for fancy horses."

"I bet he was fancy once."

"Rainbow?" I say doubtfully.

"Why not?"

"Well, he's just a pony, for one thing. Ponies aren't exactly fancy. More . . . folky."

"Folky?"

"Cute."

"Let's give him a bath tomorrow and brush him really well. And braid his mane."

"You don't want to go to the beach again?"

She rubs her tummy. "I think I need a day off."

"Good point."

Inside, my mom and dad are cooking together in the kitchen. My mom chops garlic while my dad does the onions. Only, tears are streaming down my mom's face instead of my dad's.

"Mom! What's wrong?" Ivy runs over and hugs her around the waist.

"It's just the onions," my mom says. "I can't be anywhere near them when they're getting chopped."

I catch my dad's eye, and I know my mom is lying just from the apologetic way he looks at me. I hand him the bowl of basil and keep my thoughts to myself.

My dad tosses the onions into a big pot on the stove. They sizzle when they hit the oil. "You want to stir these while I chop the basil, Rachel? And add a pinch of salt in there, too, will ya?"

He tousles my hair as he walks by.

"Ew, don't put your onion hands in my hair!" I say.

Just for that, he tousles my hair again.

"Dad!"

"Aw, relax, that was my knife hand. Nice and clean."

My mom tosses the garlic on top of the onions. "Get stirring, Rach, before the onions stick to the bottom." She wipes her eyes and half smiles at me. "You have a good day at the beach?"

"It was OK." I grab a wooden spoon and stir everything around to coat it with oil.

"Rachel and Micah are still in a fight," Ivy says. "And I ate too much junk and threw up. But now I feel better."

169

My mom looks at me and raises her eyebrows, which is her way of telling me I screwed up without yelling at me for it.

"Why are you and Micah in a fight?" my dad asks. "Does this mean the wedding plans are on hold?"

I roll my eyes and go back to stirring. I am so tired of that stupid joke.

"Micah is jealous," Ivy says.

"Jealous of what?" my mom asks.

"Ivy, maybe you should shut up now," I say.

"She said 'shut up'!" Ivy says. "Did you hear that?"

"Rachel, don't say 'shut up.' It's not nice." My mom puts a pot of water on the stove and turns on the burner. "Everything OK with you and Micah?"

I shrug.

"If you want to talk about it, I'm here," she says quietly.

"What kind of junk made you puke, buddy?" my dad asks.

Ivy begins to list all the treats she stuffed her face with while I keep stirring the onions and garlic, even though they don't need it.

My mom reaches past me and dumps in a can of stewed tomatoes, then another. I stir and stir as everyone hustles around behind me. I think about my mom's tears, and Micah not talking to me, and Cybil's comment about all of us being fluid, and how she doesn't like people based on their gender, and I wonder who she has a crush on, and—

"Hello!" calls a voice. "Anyone home?"

We all pause and look in the direction of the voice as Mr. Townsend appears in the kitchen doorway.

"Hi, neighbors!" he says.

My dad wipes his hands on his apron. "You must be Mr. Townsend. I'm Paul." He reaches out to shake hands.

"Please, call me Bev. What a lovely home you have. It's very . . . cozy."

The difference between our cramped old kitchen with the peeling linoleum floor and stained countertops and the Townsends' is pretty stark. Their sink probably cost more than what our entire kitchen is worth. But he doesn't say it in a snobby way, just observational.

"What are you stirring in there, Rachel? It smells delicious."

"Tomato sauce," I say.

"Homemade? Well, that's impressive. I don't think I've ever met a kid who knew how to cook her own sauce."

I smile. "It's not very hard."

"Team effort," my dad says. "Would you like to stay for dinner?"

My mom gives my dad a sideways glance that means he's gonna get in trouble later.

"Oh, no, no. But thank you! I just stopped by to give Rachel her check for the week."

He hands me an envelope. "I think Ferdinand was disappointed when I showed up to walk him this afternoon. He really missed you!"

"I bet Lucy didn't miss her," Ivy says.

"Lucy doesn't miss anyone. She's a pig with attitude. But not for long! Which reminds me, there's no way Greer and I will be able to use all the meat. We'd be happy to give you some pork and bacon."

Ivy gives me an urgent look, as if she expects me to speak up on Lucy's behalf.

"Oh," my mom says. "Thank you."

Ivy nudges me. This is my *Charlotte's Web* moment. But I'm no Fern. At least not tonight.

"I think she's nice," Ivy says when it becomes clear I'm no use.

"She's really not so bad," I say lamely.

"Girls, you know how farms work," my mom says.

"Are . . . are you going to kill the other animals, too?" Ivy asks, ignoring her.

"Probably some chickens, eventually," Mr. Townsend says awkwardly.

"Ivy, don't make Mr. Townsend feel uncomfortable," my mom says.

"There's nothing wrong with raising your own food," my dad says. "I'm sure that pig is having a much better life than most that are raised for meat."

Mr. Townsend smiles but looks increasingly uncomfortable. "Right. Well, I should get back home. It was nice to see you all!"

"Are you sure you can't stay?" my dad asks again.

But Mr. Townsend is already rushing out of the room.

"Have a nice weekend!" my mom calls.

I want to run after him and beg him not to kill Lucy. I start to step forward, but my mom pulls me back.

"Rachel, I know what you're up to, and you can't. Lucy is their pig, and they have every right to raise her for food."

"But—"

"Rach," my dad says. "It's farm life."

"Farm life sucks!" I yell.

"Shh. He might hear you," my mom says.

"Poor Lucy," Ivy says.

My mom pats her on the head, the way she usually pats me. "It's just the life cycle, sweetie."

"I'm not eating bacon anymore," I say.

My mom rolls her eyes at me and tests the pasta. "Grab the colander, would you, Rach? This is done."

Dinner is kind of quiet as we all think about poor Lucy's fate. My dad tries to bring up something new to talk about, but we keep circling back to raising animals. Ivy seems like she's on the verge of tears. I'm glad tonight's meal is meatless.

After dinner I offer to play a board game with Ivy. She picks Monopoly because it takes the longest. She has the worst strategy and always loses and gets upset, so tonight I decide not to buy any property until she gets a set and can put houses on something. My parents usually offer to play with us, but tonight they retreat into the dining room and talk quietly while they drink wine. Every so often one of them raises their voice and the other makes a hushing sound, then they get quiet again. I put some music on to drown out their voices, and Ivy and I sing along as we play. When Ivy finally wins, she insists that the Rolling Stones are her good-luck charm because that's what was playing when she finally made me go bankrupt. She spreads all her property on the floor and lies down on top of it singing "Jumpin' Jack Flash" at the top of her lungs while she rolls around in the money.

"Take my picture!" she insists. "I want you to send it to Micah!"

Micah is the kind of person who does not believe in letting little kids win or cheat. He's made Ivy cry a million times over games, but they always make up.

I find my phone to take a picture and send it. We wait for Micah to reply, watching as the screen says *Delivered,* then *Read.*" But Micah still doesn't send a message back. It's one thing to be a jerk to me, but it's another to ignore Ivy. He knows how excited Ivy must be about winning for the first time. Maybe he knows I let her win and doesn't think it should count.

Sometimes Micah really drives me crazy.

"Why won't he reply?" Ivy asks.

I shrug. "Who knows," I say. "Maybe you should call him."

"Really? Can I?"

She runs over to the house phone and asks me for his number.

She does a little victory dance, bumping her hips

from side to side, while she waits for Micah to answer the phone.

"Hi, Mr. Sasaki. It's Ivy. Is Micah home?"

There's a pause. I bet Micah purposefully didn't answer it when he saw our number.

"Micah! Did you get Rachel's text? I finally won Monopoly!" She starts doing another victory dance. "No, she didn't let me win!" She stops dancing. "No." She looks over at me suspiciously. "No, she didn't."

I march over to the phone and grab it away from Ivy.

"Micah! Why are you being such a jerk?"

There's silence on the other end. Ivy stares at me, her eyes filling with tears.

"He hung up," I say.

"I don't like him anymore," Ivy says. The hurt on her face makes my heart ache. I put my arm around her and give her a squeeze.

"Me either," I say quietly.

ᑫ Chapter Sixteen ᑐ

We spend the weekend helping my parents in the garden. Ivy and I clean Rainbow's stall, and then I read to them for hours while Rainbow grazes and Ivy braids his mane. He wasn't too excited about his bath and rolled in the grass as soon as we rinsed him off, but he smells better now and is a lot less dusty. I help Ivy make obstacle courses for her bike in the driveway and give her different challenges to try. We play Monopoly again and I let her win, but not quite as easily. We don't call Micah to celebrate.

Late Sunday afternoon, after we've helped weed the entire garden, my dad suggests we go for a swim. We pile in the van and drive to the beach. It's late enough that not too many people are there. My dad runs into the water wearing his dirty garden shorts, and Ivy hollers, "Charge!" as if she's heading into battle and runs in after him. My mom stands at the shoreline with her toes touching the water. She's wearing her garden clothes still, and I wonder if she even owns a bathing suit anymore.

"You going in?" I ask.

She has soil on the tip of her nose and on her left cheek. The creases in her forehead are dark where she's rubbed the dirt in when she wiped the sweat away.

"I like standing here," she says, looking back out at the water. "You go ahead and cool off."

"Mom," I say, a little hesitantly. "Are you OK?"

She doesn't answer right away. Instead, she cranes her neck as if she's trying to see something in the distance, far beyond the rope line. I feel a worry that's been deep inside me turn into an ache. Seeing her like this scares me. It shouldn't take her so long to answer.

"Life's just challenging sometimes," she finally says. "But we'll manage." The more she says this phrase, the more it sounds like she doesn't believe it anymore.

She touches the side of my face in her gentle way. "I promise," she says, as if she knows I'm not so sure.

Her reassuring hand makes the ache slip back where it was, even if it feels temporary.

"I wish you'd come in the water. It's fun!"

"Maybe in a bit. You go on."

I join my dad and Ivy. We teach my dad how to play Clueless, but he's kind of useless at it. Then we race to the rope line and back. My mom stays at the water's edge, watching us. Or watching beyond us. As if she's trying to see the future somewhere far out from shore.

"Come on in, Mom!" Ivy yells.

She waves as if she can't really hear what Ivy's saying.

My dad glances over at my mom and makes a worried face, but quickly turns away when he sees me notice.

"Can I jump off your shoulders?" Ivy asks him.

He dunks under the water and Ivy tries to get her feet up on his shoulders, but she's a lot bigger than the last time she did this with him, and my dad struggles to stand back up. I try to help, but Ivy falls backward on top of me. We try a bunch more times, but then Ivy gets water up her nose and my dad's shoulders are bright red from all the slipping and sliding and we finally give up.

We float on our backs and look up at the sky, which seems to be getting increasingly cloudy.

I don't know why my parents never take us

swimming in the summer like this. I guess they're always too busy or too tired. But this is nice. It's almost perfect.

I look back to shore again, and my mom is gone. I search the whole beach for her but don't see her. Then, finally, I see a lone swimmer at the far end of the beach, swimming along the rope line. She's doing the crawl, lifting her head for a breath with every other stroke. She glides through the water with grace. I can tell she's wearing her T-shirt and shorts. I must've been right about the bathing suit. I don't point her out to Ivy and my dad, who are busy floating on their backs, sharing Monopoly strategies. Instead, I quietly swim out to her.

We swim side by side along the rope line, my mom not really acknowledging me, and me not really acknowledging her. I try to copy her strokes and keep up with her. When we get to the far corner, we stop and tread water to catch our breath.

"It does feel good," she finally says. She smiles at me again and dunks her head underwater to get her hair out of her face. The dirt has washed off, and she looks less tired.

"So . . . do you want to tell me what's going on with Micah?" she asks.

I turn away from her and scan the beach again. The only people left are an older couple sitting in camp chairs pulled up to the edge of the water so they can dip their toes in. A little dog circles them, yapping for their attention. The lifeguard is gone because it's after hours, so no one can kick the dog off the beach.

"It's a little complicated," I say.

"Did something happen at the party? It seems that's the last time you two were together."

The little dog jumps in the water and splashes the old people. The man waves a cane at the dog and tells it to sit. The dog just yaps again.

"I'm embarrassed to tell you," I say. "It was something really stupid, and I regret it a lot."

"Oh, Rachel. I'm sorry."

We keep treading water, watching the couple with the dog. It feels different here, with nowhere to go, and nothing to do but talk and be together. It feels nice.

"I kissed a boy," I tell her. Something about being alone with her like this makes me feel safe to share secrets.

Her eyes widen in surprise. "You did?"

"I wasn't really expecting to. It just happened."

"Was it Micah?"

Of course she would think it was Micah.

"No," I say. My throat tightens the way it always does when I'm about to cry. "That's the problem. It was this other boy who I was talking with in the pool. We were just talking about school and what classes we have next fall and . . . then I could tell he was about to kiss me, and I let him. And Micah saw and got really mad."

"Poor Micah. He's so in love with you."

"Don't say that!" I say too loudly. "Everyone says that, and it makes me feel terrible. I can't force myself to like someone, Mom. I can't help it if I don't have feelings for him."

"I'm sorry, honey. I didn't mean to make you feel bad. You shouldn't."

"But I do," I say. We tread water awkwardly now, not really looking at each other.

The dog jumps up in the old woman's lap and she shrieks, but then laughs.

The old man says something I can't quite hear. It sounds like *dumb dog*.

"What happened with the boy you kissed?" my mom finally asks.

"Nothing. I made it clear I wasn't interested, and he left me alone. But it doesn't matter because Micah is still mad at me and he hasn't replied to my texts and I'm afraid we aren't friends anymore."

"Oh, no, he'll come around. He's just confused."

I want to tell her so am I. I want to tell her I don't understand why I can't seem to feel anything when it comes to boys but I feel funny around Cybil. I want to tell her I don't know what this means, but I think I know and it scares me even though it shouldn't.

"Don't worry so much, Rachel. Things will be OK. Micah is sensitive. You know that. And you've had fights before and always made up."

"This is different," I say. "*He's* different. And . . . *I'm* different."

But she doesn't seem to understand what I mean, and I don't feel brave enough, or sure enough, to explain.

I feel so lonely all of a sudden. Like I don't have a single friend in the world. I feel mad at Micah for putting me in this awkward place. It's not fair. It makes me feel like I'm doing something wrong even though I know I'm not. Instead of crying, I feel like screaming.

"He's such a jerk!" I say. "I hate boys."

My mom looks over at my dad and sister.

"Except for Dad," I say.

She half smiles. "It sounds like Micah is being a jerk.

You're right. And I really hope you can work it out and be friends again."

I don't know what makes me do it, but I fill my mouth with water and squirt it at her. It's something Ivy would do, not me. My mom looks shocked at first, then starts to laugh. She fills her own mouth and spits at me. It's the silliest thing, but for some reason, it seems we both needed to do something unexpected to break this horrible feeling that ruined our special time together.

"Hey!" Ivy calls, and starts swimming toward us.

The magic between us floats away, and I wish I could reach for it and hold tight. I wish my mom could always be like this. Willing to be silly and play with me. But as my dad swims behind Ivy, I can feel the seriousness slide back between us, pushing the lightness down deep.

Back at home, we boil some pasta to have with the leftover tomato sauce and play Yahtzee with the Rolling Stones in the background for luck. Ivy gets two Yahtzees and wins the game. "I'm on a winning streak!" she tells us, getting up to do her victory dance. "Who wants to play Monopoly next?"

My parents exchange a look and back away from the table.

"Aw, come on, you're just afraid to lose!" Ivy whines.

"I'll play with you," I say.

She jumps up and down and runs to get the box.

"You're a good sister," my dad tells me.

My mom rubs my back before she and my dad disappear into the other room with new glasses of wine. I wonder if this means I'm too old for head pats now.

Ivy and I set up the game while we listen to music coming from the living room. I turn down the Rolling Stones so I can hear. It's Elvis, singing about falling in love, and I know my parents are dancing in there. Holding each other close.

"Let's roll at the same time to see who goes first," Ivy says.

I get a six, and she gets a three. She frowns and pushes the dice at me in a way-too-babyish gesture. "It's because you turned down my music," she says.

"Don't be a baby," I tell her.

This time, I don't let her win.

Before I follow Ivy into the living room to say good night to my parents, I find my paycheck from Mr. Townsend and sign the back. Then I rip a sheet of paper off the shopping-list pad we keep on the fridge and fold it over the check and draw a heart on it. *For groceries,* I write under the heart. I leave it on top of my mom's purse and turn off the light.

৬ Chapter Seventeen ৩

Everyone seems happy to see me when I go back to work on Monday morning—except for the chickens. Poor little Bashful is on the outskirts as usual, so I make sure to toss her some extra feed while the others are busy.

I save Lucy for last. She lifts her head and blinks when she sees me. My heart hurts, thinking about her future.

"I was supposed to love the hell out of you," I say. "But I can't even save you."

She eyes me suspiciously.

"I have your breakfast," I tell her. "Are you going to let me set it out for you, or are you going to do your body-slam nonsense?"

She rolls her body a little, rocking back and forth until she gets on her feet, then takes a few steps toward me.

"Hi," I say. "How are you feeling?"

She shifts her weight from one hoof to the other.

I climb up on the railing.

Lucy takes another step.

I lift her feed bucket slowly up over the top rail.

"Stay," I tell her, as if she's a dog. "Wait."

She sniffs. Her pink snout is wet and has bits of sawdust on it. She blinks her long pink eyelashes at me.

"Stay," I say again, slowly lowering the pail down on her side of the pen.

She begins to trot toward me, picking up speed.

I slip the handle of the bucket onto its hook and jump off the fence before Lucy reaches me.

"Stay!" I yell again. She stops in her tracks and lifts her head to sniff again.

"Good girl!" I yell. She trots up to the bucket and looks inside, then starts to eat.

"See? All you had to do was wait. You didn't waste a single drop this time!"

Lucy ignores me and keeps eating. I wait for her to finish so I can retrieve the dirty bucket. When she's done, she lifts her face to me and grunts.

"You're welcome," I say.

She turns and flicks her tail as she walks over to her corner, then flops down in the sun.

I reach over the railing and take her bucket.

"We're going to be friends soon!" I call to her. But then I remember her days are numbered. And the more we become friends, the harder it's going to be to say good-bye.

"You're not all bad," I tell her. "I bet you're nothing like Mr. Townsend's sister-in-law."

She watches me for a little while, as if she's considering whether or not that's true. The longer I stand here, the worse I feel. "I really do wish I could save you," I tell her.

She grunts, rolls over, and closes her eyes.

Before I cross the street, a car I don't recognize pulls out of our driveway. I start to wave, but the driver seems to look the other way from me on purpose. When I go in, my mom is sitting at the dining-room table with a thick envelope in front of her and her back is shaking the way a person's back shakes when they are sobbing so hard no sounds come out.

My dad's van wasn't in the driveway. They should both have left for work by now.

"Mom?" I ask quietly.

I can hear SpongeBob whining on the TV in the other room.

I step closer. "Mom? Why aren't you at work? Where's Dad?"

She doesn't seem to hear me. Her back keeps shaking, as if her whole body is revving up to let out the loudest cry ever.

My heart begins to beat faster, but it feels like more than a hummingbird trapped in my chest. It feels like a woodpecker.

I stand behind my mom. The letter looks very official. At the top it says THE PEOPLE'S BANK in green ink. The words *Notice of Acceleration* are typed in big bold letters. And below that, something about foreclosure.

I've heard my mom say the word *foreclosure* when she and my dad fight about money, and it always sounds like this possible threat. Something about the house. But my dad always comforts her and tells her banks don't like to do that. They help people find a way to avoid it.

But here it is. A letter with that word.

The woodpecker in my chest seems to have made a gaping hole in it, but instead of everything spilling out of me, I feel like I'm falling into myself, into some dark place I can feel but not see. This must be what my mom feels, too. Her face is all scrunched up like a newborn baby's, still stuck in that silent moment before the howling comes.

"Mom," I say again.

She turns in her chair and reaches for me. I move closer so she can grab on. She squeezes my body to her, hiding her face in the front of my grimy T-shirt.

I get one arm free and gently pat her head the way she used to pat mine.

Her back rises up as she takes a deep breath, and then she sobs into the hole in my chest, my punctured heart. She sobs and sobs, but the sound is muffled in my shirt. I hold tight to her as she presses her face into me. My T-shirt slowly dampens with her tears. My own tears drip down off my cheeks into her messy hair.

In the distance, SpongeBob laughs and squeals. I blink my tears back, knowing that if Ivy comes in the room right now and sees my mom like this, it will scare her. I rub my mom's back to try to calm her down. Around us, the papers strewn all over the table — mostly unpaid bills and unread newspapers — seem to have lost their importance. On the far wall behind the table, portraits of Ivy and me standing on the front steps of the house on the first day of school, a bittersweet wreath on the door behind us in nearly every picture, stare back at me. In kindergarten, I'm all by myself. I'm wearing uneven braids, a pink T-shirt, jeans, and red rubber boots. I loved those boots because Paddington Bear wore them and he was my favorite. My mother had made me toast with marmalade for breakfast that morning, just like Paddington ate. I remember crying the night before because I didn't want to leave the house. I loved playing in the backyard in the sandpile my dad made for me, where all my trucks and cars and my mom's old Fisher-Price people sat waiting for me to build them a new village and roads in the sand. The house was all I knew, and everything about it seemed magical to me. But my mom, who was nine months pregnant with Ivy and whose giant belly pressed into me when she hugged me, had promised school would be magical, too.

The next year, I'm holding roly-poly Ivy in my arms. I'm wearing my favorite sundress and crying in the picture. So is Ivy. This time, I didn't want to go to school because I didn't want to leave Ivy. I was convinced she needed me more than she needed my mom. I don't even remember now why I thought that. But I had helped make her nursery out of the old attic we'd renovated; it was next to my bedroom and much closer to my room than my parents' room downstairs. I was always the first one to hear her crying. Sometimes I'd carry her down to my mom in the middle of the night to nurse.

In the third picture, I'm headed off to second grade and Ivy is standing next to me. This time, I look thrilled to go to school, but Ivy is in tears again, tugging at the hem of my shirt as if she thought she was strong enough to keep me there.

The pictures go on and on, year after year, showing how we grew apart and together again, all on those front steps of our house.

When my mom finally stops crying, she slowly pulls her head away from me. My shirt is damp with her tears and runny nose stuff. My mom squeezes my shoulders but doesn't look up.

She takes a deep breath. Then another.

"We're losing the house?" I ask quietly.

She nods.

"Forever?"

She nods again.

I stare at the first-day-of-school pictures again. At the wallpaper behind them. I remember helping my mom research what pattern to get, and figuring out what the walls would have looked like when the house was built, back in the 1800s. I learned how to measure and cut the strips of paper, wet them with a special sponge, then help my parents set each one on the wall just so. The wallpaper looked old-fashioned and strange, but it made the house feel special. Like we were living in a museum.

Through the years, my parents lovingly repaired each room in this house. Fixing walls, caulking windows, reshingling the roof, scraping and painting the outside for hours in the hot summer sun. This was supposed to be the house they never left. They used to say someday Ivy and I would bring our own children here, to visit their grandparents.

This place is more than a house; it's a family member. We *can't* live anywhere else. It's part of us.

My mom wipes her face with the sleeve of her shirt. Carefully she folds the notice and puts it back inside the envelope.

"What if we go to the bank and ask for more time?" I ask. "I could get another job. I could babysit the Grayson twins. Or—"

"We've tried all that," my mom says quietly. "This is it."

She stands slowly, like an old person. I guess she

knew it was coming. I guess this is what she was thinking about when she stood at the water's edge last night. It's why she didn't go to work with my dad. Because she knew the woman from the bank was coming.

"Mom," I say. "There has to be something we can do."

She doesn't turn around. She lifts her hand as if to silence me, then goes into her bedroom and shuts the door.

"What's going on?" Ivy asks. She stands in the doorway between the kitchen and dining room. She's wearing a T-shirt with a surprised emoji face on it and just her underwear.

"Put some shorts on," I tell her.

"It's too hot."

"Well, you look gross," I say.

She turns and shakes her butt at me. Her worn undies have a hole in one cheek.

I have a terrible urge to kick her. But when she turns around and says, "Why are you crying?" I brush her off and say, "It's nothing."

She follows me as I climb the stairs to my room.

"What's wrong, Rachel? Did Micah break up with you as friends?"

"Shut up," I say.

"What's your problem? Why are you being so mean?"

"Just put some shorts on!" I yell. I slam my bedroom door in her face.

She pounds on it from the other side. "You're a jerk!" she yells.

"Get used to it!" I yell back.

George is sleeping on my bed. He looks up at me groggily and stands on shaky legs. I sit next to him and cry harder. He rubs against my arm for a pat. I lie down, and he steps up on my chest, purring like mad. My window is open, and the paper lantern swings in the breeze. The light-blue curtains my mom made dance happily as the air passes through. I think of the first day of summer and how hopeful it all felt. What a lie. Why is life always changing for the worse?

I reach for my old teddy bear and press him over my face so I can scream into his belly the way my mom sobbed into mine. George jumps down and meows at my door. I scream again, but it doesn't make me feel any better. People always say to cry harder or yell louder to let it all out, but that's just a stupid phrase. Crying and screaming don't make your sadness go away. They just make you feel it even more.

George meows again, and then I hear my door open.

"Rach?" Ivy asks quietly.

I want to yell at her for opening my door without knocking, but why bother?

"I'm just letting the cat out," she says.

The door closes again.

I roll over on my side and look at all the photos taped to my wall. When Micah and I first got our phones, we took a million stupid selfies together and printed them at his house. Then we cut them out and made collages, adding to them every time we did something new. A year's worth of Micah selfies stare back at me. We're smiling or laughing or making funny faces in every single one. Most of them are taken in my room or in the backyard. There are some with Rainbow, who doesn't look amused. I realize with a horrible jolt that if we have to leave here, we'll have to find a place for him. If we have to leave here, where will we go? I get up and pull a picture of Rainbow off the door and start crying all over again. What will happen to him? What will happen to us?

I find my phone and text Micah.

I have to talk to you. This is really important.

I wait until I see that he's read the message. No response.

Micah, this is serious.

I wait again.

We're . . . I pause. If I text the words, they'll be true. This won't be some dream or misunderstanding. This will really be happening.

I delete *We're.*

The bank foreclosed on our house.

I stare at the words before I press the send button.

They seem so formal. So awful. So real.

I press.

My phone rings seconds after.

"What are you talking about?" Micah asks.

"We got the letter today."

"But what does it mean?"

"It means the bank is taking the house away from us. We have to move."

He's quiet, but I can hear him breathing. His breaths get faster as the truth sinks in.

"But . . . that . . . are you sure?"

"Yes."

"But . . . it's not fair. There has to be a way."

"I don't think so," I say. "I think my parents have run out of ways."

"Can I come over?" he asks.

"Yes, please."

The phone goes quiet. I press the picture of Rainbow to my heart.

I let it all out.

And I'm right.

I don't feel any better. I just feel the hurt even more.

ᐰ Chapter Eighteen ᐱ

"When something terrible happens, people say they wish they could go back in time to prevent it. But how can you know what really caused it in the first place?" Micah says this without looking at me. His hair hasn't been washed. I can tell because it has sleep dents in it and it seems a little greasy. His hair always takes on a sheen when he waits too long to wash it. It almost looks wet. I bet it smells.

I hate myself for thinking that. But right now I kind of also hate him. Why do people always say dumb stuff when they're trying to make you feel better? I want him to be more angry than me. I want him to be angry *for* me.

But he's trying to be calm because he thinks that's what I need.

His hair is disgusting.

"When is it going to happen?" he asks, not looking at me.

It feels uncomfortable to be with him like this after everything that's happened. We're sitting on the grass in the backyard. Rainbow grazes nearby. Every so often he swishes his tail to make the flies go away, but they always come back.

"Soon, I think."

"How soon?"

"I don't know!" I snap.

Micah closes his mouth, but his jaw moves like he's biting his teeth together so he won't yell. His eyes get glassy, as if he's about to cry. I would tell him to let it all out, but honestly it is the last thing I want.

I start to care less about his hair, though.

"Where will you go?" he asks quietly.

"I don't know."

He turns away so I can't see his face. There's an extra-big hair dent on the back of his head. His shoulders tremble. Now that I see how much he's hurting, I want to reach out and pat the dent away, even if his hair is gross. I want to hug him. I want to press my face into his shirt and cry into him.

A big ball of despair rises up my throat, like a giant sob just waiting to explode out of me.

Micah turns back to me and hugs me, and then I do sob, all over his chest. I soak his T-shirt with my tears, claiming it. He squeezes harder and cries into the top of my head.

"I'm sorry," he says. "I'm sorry this is really happening. I'm sorry I was such a jerk. And for not returning your texts." He is letting it all out.

This feels like a bad dream that you can't wake up from. The kind of dream that's turning into not quite a nightmare, but something worse. The kind where things start happening that are totally out of your control and suddenly you realize it's just a dream but you can't wake up. You tell yourself to open your eyes and you'll be safe in your bed and all the sadness won't be real, but when you open them, you're still in this other, horrible place and things keep getting worse, and sadder, and more desperate.

There was this storybook my mom read to me when I was a kid about a family who has calamitous things happen to them. Each time something awful happens, the grandfather yells out, "Could be worse!" and then the worse thing happens. But they keep making the best of it somehow, even though things actually do get worse and worse. I think "Could be worse!" is the meanest thing someone could say to a person who's hurting.

"Everything's too out of control," I say. "I don't know how I'm supposed to feel."

"Maybe there are too many feelings to have about this. I mean, I'd be angry. And sad. And scared. And . . ."

"All of those things," I say.

"Maybe just pick one for now, and deal with that."

"Sad," I say.

His eyes water a little, and I feel mine do the same again.

"Everything's going to be different now. We won't be neighbors anymore."

"But we'll still be together forever," Micah says. "I promise I'll never be a jerk again."

"I was a jerk, too," I say. "I'm sorry."

We're quiet for a little while. I try to take slow, deep breaths to make the ache in my throat go away, but it doesn't help.

"I hate this so much." The minute I think about having to leave, an avalanche of all the other things that means I'll lose comes careening at me. The house. My bedroom. The barn. My job. The backyard. The stone-wall houses. Family dinner-making in the kitchen. Riding bikes in the driveway. The first-day-of-school pictures. The bittersweet wreaths. Ivy and I were both born here. We *belong* here.

"We have to make a pact not to let this change us," Micah says. He holds out his hand. "Put yours on top of mine."

I reach out and put my hand on his. My friend-ship bracelet has gotten worn, but it still looks pretty. Micah's hand is warm and rough. He puts his other hand on top of mine so mine is trapped inside. Instead of saying anything, we just look at each other and hold on.

"Don't let go," he says quietly.

"I won't," I say.

"I mean even when I walk away, I'll still be holding on. I always will."

"Me too."

We relax and my hand slips from his grasp, but I don't feel like we let go. I feel like we are reconnected forever.

We lean back on the ground and listen to Rainbow nibble bits of grass. I think not knowing what's going to happen to him is even worse than not knowing what's going to happen to me. Another tear leaks out the side of my eye. Then another. I don't reach up to wipe them away, because I don't want Micah to look at me and see that I'm crying again. So we both lie here, listening to Rainbow, quietly wondering what's going to happen to all of us.

꒰ Chapter Nineteen ꒱

When Ivy finds us out back, both of our faces tear-soaked, she knows something's up.

"What's going on?" she asks. "Mom locked herself in her bedroom and won't come out. And you guys are crying. It's not because you broke up, is it? It's something worse."

She has raspberry jam on the front of her shirt, and her bare legs are covered with dirt and scabs.

"Have you had a bath since the last time I checked?" I ask, trying to change the subject.

"I don't need a bath. We just went to the beach last night, remember?"

"How did you get so dirty in such a short time?"

Ivy shrugs. "I've got a new project going."

"What kind of project?"

"A hole."

"For what?"

"To get cool in. Do you know that's why dogs dig sometimes? They dig a hole and sleep in it to stay cool."

"Where did you dig this hole? How big is it?"

"Don't worry about that. Just trust me that you'll thank me next time it gets really hot. And stop changing the subject. Please tell me what's going on."

Rainbow comes up behind her and nuzzles her grubby hand. Ivy absently rubs his velvety muzzle but keeps her eyes on me.

"I don't know much," I say. "So what I tell you won't be the full story, and you're going to have a lot of questions I can't answer. But we'll find out soon."

She nods.

"An official letter came from the bank today."

"Is it about the house and the bills?"

"Yes."

She nods again. "We can't afford to stay in the house, can we?" she says quietly.

"No."

Her lower lip quivers.

"Ivy, it's going to be OK."

She shakes her head. "No, it's not."

"Yes. We aren't sick. We aren't dying. We're losing our house."

The words sound pathetic. Putting things in perspective is supposed to help. So why does this still feel just as dire as being horribly sick? What if we become homeless? What if we lose everything?

Ivy wobbles on her spindly legs as the grief settles into her body. She looks around the yard, and back toward the house, and then at Rainbow.

"But what will happen to us?" she asks. "What will happen to Rainbow?"

"I don't know," I say.

"Where will we go?"

"I don't know."

"What about George?"

"I'm not sure."

She starts to blubber. Micah gets up and hugs her. Ivy wraps her arms around Micah's waist and squeezes. She cries into Micah's chest like my mom did to me. Her cries are high-pitched, like a kitten. Like a baby.

I get up and join the hug. I don't cry, though. Somehow Ivy's tears keep me from showing mine. Micah's cheek presses against mine as we squeeze Ivy between us.

"You'll be all right," Micah says quietly. "I promise."

But I don't know if Ivy hears him through her cries. We hold her until she finally quiets and stops squeezing Micah. When we step apart, we all look at one another awkwardly, as if we have to get used to our new relationship. Micah, the lucky one. Ivy and me, the unluckies.

"Maybe we should go to the beach," Micah says.

Ivy looks at me for approval. Part of me doesn't want to leave the house again, knowing our time here is almost over. Shouldn't we spend every last minute here that we can?

But another part of me thinks that walking back into the house and seeing my mom's closed door, seeing everything we are about to lose, will hurt more.

"Let's be quick," I say to Ivy, pulling our towels and bathing suits from the clothesline.

"I'll meet you in the driveway," Micah says.

We hurry inside and change as fast as we can. I leave a note on the dining-room table telling my mom we're going to the beach with Micah. It feels strange to write the note, and I wonder if it would be better to stay home in case she needs me. But that's silly, and backward, too. She's the mom, not me.

I end the note with an *I love you* and a heart. It makes me think of the *Home Is Where the Heart Is* pillow.

If home is where the heart is, what happens when you lose your home?

"C'mon!" Ivy says, tugging on my backpack.

"OK, OK," I say.

Micah is waiting for us in the driveway with our bikes ready to go. I don't know why it feels like we're running away when we turn onto the road, but it does.

The beach is quiet today. The weather is a bit overcast and looks like rain. As we pass the lifeguard stand, the lifeguard tells us we'll have to get out of the water immediately if it starts to thunder. She seems annoyed to have to be here on such a yucky day.

We toss our stuff at our usual place at the far end of the beach and stand with our toes in the water.

"Will we still get to come here after we move?" Ivy asks.

"Of course," says Micah. "It's not like you're moving out of town."

When he says it, I realize that might not be true. What if we can't find a place here to live? Because my dad's a real-estate agent, he talks about rent and mortgages all the time, and how, around here, it's actually cheaper to have a mortgage than to pay rent. So if we can't afford to pay our mortgage, how will we pay rent somewhere? There's only one apartment complex for people with low incomes that I know of in town, and I don't know how often they have apartments available. I've only been there once. A classmate had a birthday party when I was in the first or second grade. The rooms were small, and the carpet smelled funny. The kid's name was Charlie, and I remember how I was jealous because he had two bunk beds in his room, which he shared with his two brothers and little sister. I remember wishing I had more siblings and we could all sleep in the same room like that. I thought it would be cozy, and I'd never be afraid of the dark because I wouldn't be alone.

"Let's go in. I'm hot!" Ivy says. "Race you to the line!"

Micah starts to chase after her but stops when I don't follow.

"You coming?"

I shrug. "I'm too cold. Go ahead."

He smiles at me before he turns to join Ivy. I force myself to smile back. No, not force. It actually comes naturally. I'm so relieved we're friends again. Especially now. But as I watch him easily catch up to Ivy but let her win, I know things are never going to be the same. He never lets Ivy win races, just like he never lets her win at Monopoly. It's because he feels sorry for her now. I don't know why, but it annoys me. I don't want him to treat us differently.

Micah has never had to feel self-conscious wearing clothes from a local thrift shop, worrying that someone might recognize them as a sibling's old jeans or whatever. He's never had to wonder if there will be real food for dinner or if he'll have to help his parents "get creative" with what's in the cupboards and make up funny, fancy names for crazy concoctions, like Tuna al Dente Saltino for saltine crackers and canned tuna fish that was on sale because the can was dented.

When I eat at Micah's, we have fish that doesn't come in a can and fresh-baked bread from a bakery, not from a plastic bag on the discount shelf in the grocery store. That's just normal for Micah. Sometimes I wonder why he wants to spend so much time at our house when things are so much nicer at his.

"Rachel!" a voice calls from the far end of the beach.

Cybil runs toward me.

"Hi! I tried texting you but you didn't answer, so I called your house and your mom told me you were here," she says, all out of breath. "I hope it's OK that Sam gave me your number. Um, are you OK?"

"What?"

She reaches toward my face and brushes my cheek with her fingers. "You're crying?"

"I am?" I wipe my eyes with my palms. How do you cry without even realizing it?

"You and Micah aren't still fighting, are you?"

"No," I say quietly. "We made up."

She waits for me to explain my tears, but I don't know how, so we stand there, our toes in the water, watching Micah and Ivy. She is so close to me that I can feel the warmth of her arm next to mine, almost touching but not.

"Micah's nice," she finally says, as if she's come to that conclusion after watching him play so patiently with Ivy.

"He is," I say.

"But he's just your friend. Not your boyfriend?"

"Just my friend."

"Good."

She leans closer to me so that our arms are touching. I feel a funny energy run through my arm. I don't dare turn to look at her.

"I really like you, Rachel," she says, leaning even closer so that the length of her arm is pressed against the length of mine.

"I like you, too," I say automatically.

Her fingers reach to lace with mine and my heart feels just the way it did all those years ago when Micah held my hand under the lilac bushes. We stand there stock-still, me not daring to move, her not wanting to, I suppose, until Micah and Ivy start to swim toward us. Then we automatically step apart, as if we were doing something wrong and don't want to get caught. The slight breeze against my arm feels cold where she isn't touching me anymore.

My best friend has always been a boy. I've never had a close girl friend. Do girl friends hold hands? Or is this something else?

My heart is still racing when Micah reaches us. He gives me a funny look.

"Hey, Cybil," he says. "What are you doing here?"

"Oh," she says, "I totally forgot. Sierra's having another party and I came to invite"—she pauses as if she realizes she was about to say the wrong thing—"you guys," she finishes.

"Cool," Micah says. "Right?" he asks me.

"Yeah," I say. "Cool." I guess. The ghost of Cybil's hand in mine lingers.

"Great!" Cybil says. "Well, I have to get back to work. I'm on my lunch break, and my dad is gonna kill me for being gone so long."

"You work for your dad?" Micah asks.

"Yeah, kind of. He's the manager at the pharmacy, and they hired me to stock shelves and stuff. It's the most boring job on the planet, but at least the pharmacy is air-conditioned. Not that it matters today. So, I'll see you guys at the party? I'll text Rachel when I know more about the time and stuff. See ya!"

She runs back down the beach. If Micah saw our fingers laced together, he doesn't say anything. I wonder if she was just trying to be kind because she knew I was sad or if she was trying to tell me . . . maybe she *likes* me? Like the way she liked Sam?

Could I like her that way, too?

I sit on my towel next to Micah and Ivy and watch the clouds thicken over the water. We forgot to pack anything to eat and our stomachs all rumble a little from time to time, but none of us admits we're hungry. Not even Ivy, who always complains.

There's no one left on the beach besides the lifeguard. She glances over at us every so often as if she hopes we'll leave.

A drop of rain splats on my knee. Then another. Ivy holds out her hand and waits. After a minute or two, a drip hits her palm. She leans her head back and sticks her tongue out.

"Have you ever gone swimming in the rain?" Micah asks.

"Nope," I say.

"Let's try!" Ivy says.

We jump up and run into the water. The lifeguard blows her whistle and shouts, "If I hear thunder, you have to get out!"

"We know!" Micah calls. He dives under the water, and Ivy and I follow. We swim to where it's over our heads and bob in the water as the rain picks up and causes ripples on the surface.

I dip under and open my eyes to watch the rain from below. It's so beautiful, water piercing water. I pop up to tell Micah and Ivy to go under and watch. The three of us dunk under and stare up at the surface of the water. Ivy's eyes bulge in wonder as the drips land gracefully above us. Every time I have to go up for air, I feel regret. I wish I could stay under here for hours, in the reassuring silence. It feels so safe under here, as if we're in some underwater world no one else knows about.

After a while, we lie on our backs and float and let the rain land on us. We keep giggling for no reason. It seems like years since I did that. Just giggled because of the wonder of something.

"Let's make a star," Micah says. He directs us to put

our heads near each other and then hold hands, spreading our legs out wide. I don't think we look much like a star, but it's fun to hold on to one another like this as the rain splashes our faces. I feel special. I know we aren't the only ones who've ever done this, but being alone out here, with no one else to see us but the grumpy lifeguard, I feel like we are experiencing something that's just for us. Something that we'll remember, no matter what happens after this terrible day.

The lifeguard's whistle blows again, and she waves at us to come in.

We listen for thunder when we get back to the beach but don't hear anything.

"She's no fun," Ivy says grumpily.

"She's just jealous," Micah says.

"We should go," I say.

We stuff our wet towels into our backpacks and walk up the beach.

"Have a good day," Ivy calls to the lifeguard as we pass by. "And I don't mean that sarcastically!"

"Gee, thanks," the lifeguard says sarcastically.

Micah cracks up, and we all run to our bikes.

I grab his hand and stop him.

"What?" he asks.

"Thanks for coming here with us," I say. "It was nice to forget for a while."

He smiles, a little sadly. "That's what friends do."

I smile a little sadly back. "Right."

"C'mon, you guys!" Ivy yells. "Let's go home!"

Home is where the heart is, I think again.

For now, anyway.

❧ Chapter Twenty ☙

It's hard to ride our bikes as the rain picks up and pounds the pavement. I squint to try and see. We finally pull over and drag our bikes under a big pine tree to wait for the rain to let up.

"This is wild!" Ivy says excitedly. "I love adventures."

"You're a goofball," Micah tells her.

Ivy does a strange little dance and then toots.

"Seriously?" I ask her. "Nice touch."

"It was my Lucy interpretation," she says.

I start to laugh and then remember that the Townsends' animals are outside in this rain!

"We have to get back *now*!" I say, after telling them what I've done.

"They'll be fine," Micah says. "A little water isn't going to hurt them."

But I feel panic rising in my chest. "I'm going to get in so much trouble if Mr. Townsend finds out!"

"Rachel, relax. Most animals get left out in the rain all the time."

"But not *these* animals. They're pampered! And what if it starts to thunder?"

"Rachel, it's OK. We can't do anything about it now. The rain will pass in a few minutes."

I pace impatiently, thinking about the horses and the goats and the sheep's wool getting all wet and poor Lucy's pen getting muddier and muddier. My chest gets tighter, and I start to have trouble breathing.

"I feel weird," I say, struggling to breathe.

Ivy stops dancing and looks worried. Micah puts his hands on my shoulders. "Breathe in slowly," he says. "I think you're having a panic attack."

I try to breathe in slowly, but my heart is racing and it's hard to catch my breath.

"Nothing is going to happen to the animals," Micah says. "They will get wet, and they might not like it, but they'll get over it. Breathe out."

I breathe out, my heart still beating way too fast.

"As soon as it stops pouring, Ivy and I will go with you and help you take care of everyone. It's going to be fine. Keep breathing."

I take a bunch of deep breaths, letting each one out slowly, and start to calm down. The rain begins to find its way through the pine boughs and drips on our heads, through the holes in our bike helmets. I concentrate on the cool water soaking my hair.

"Are you feeling better?" Micah asks.

I nod, even though I'm not sure.

When cars drive by, they splash waves of water near our feet. Ivy keeps jumping out and splashing in the puddles, then dashing back under the branches when a car comes. "I bet my cooling-off hole is turning into a swimming hole!" she says excitedly.

I concentrate on my breathing, but it doesn't help very much. My thoughts race between what's going to happen to our family and whether the animals will be OK in the rain.

When the rain finally lets up, we race to the Townsends' house. We drop our bikes in the driveway and toss our helmets on the ground, then run behind the house and down to the barns, slipping on the wet grass as we go.

We're still wearing our bathing suits and the air has gotten colder, but I hardly notice I'm so worried about everyone, even though the rain is barely a drizzle now.

"See?" Micah says when we reach Ben and Gil. "They're fine."

The gentle horses look at us in their bored sort of way and keep nuzzling the ground for grass, as if it's not even raining. Still, I run into the barn and put some grain in their buckets to coax them inside, and they happily follow.

Micah hops the fence and latches their stall gates closed.

Next we find the sheep, who are huddled against each other in the corner of their pen, but once I put a bucket of grain in their shelter, they trot happily over to me and settle inside. "Hey, Ewe," I say, petting his head.

"I thought that was Me," Micah says, coming in to help.

"Not this again," I say.

He grins. "I can't help it."

When Ferdinand sees us, he starts bucking and scratching his hooves in the mud as if he's challenging us to a tussle. "Want to walk him?" I ask Ivy. She runs for the leash and lets Ferdinand chase her around the farmyard while Micah and I let everyone else in to shelter if they want to. The chickens cluck nervously when we get close.

"What's wrong with that little one?" Micah asks, pointing to Bashful.

"She's different," I say. "They never let her eat, but I make sure she gets her share."

"I wonder why they don't like her," he says. "Maybe she's sick. Animals seem to know when someone in their group isn't well."

"I don't think she's sick. I just think they don't like her."

"Do chickens have opinions?"

"It seems so."

The rain has completely stopped now. We watch Bashful wander around by herself, picking at worms that have come out during the rain. I toss her some feed, and she races over to snatch it up before the others can. They look mad at her when they run over and there's nothing left, but they wander back to the other side of the pen again, pecking and clucking as if they're all talking to one another.

"I'm sure they're sharing their opinions right now," Micah says. "Listen to them."

"Oh, that little Bashful thinks she's so great," I say in my best chicken voice.

"I wish I had a worm burger," Micah says in a high-pitched chicken voice.

"You need a worm burger like I need my feathers plucked," I say.

We go on like this for a while, making up some babble for the chickens. It feels good to be a little silly for a change.

"Rachel! Come quick!" Ivy calls.

Micah and I stop our chicken talk and look for Ivy. She and Ferdinand are standing outside Lucy's pen. Ferdinand has his head pressed between two rungs of the fence and appears to be licking Lucy's snout.

"I thought something was wrong!" I tell her grumpily.

"Ferdinand found a girlfriend," Ivy says.

"I think she's a little old for you," Micah tells Ferdinand.

"I guess opposites really do attract," I say.

"Gross," says Ivy.

She pulls Ferdinand's head back by tugging on the lead. "C'mon, buddy, enough of that stuff."

Lucy steps close to the fence as if she wants more Ferdinand kisses.

"You sure have had a change in personality," I tell her. "Are you trying to change the Townsends' minds? If I were a spider, I'd spin you a web and write I LOVE LUCY."

She grunts at me.

"Sheesh. That's the thanks I get for caring?"

Micah reaches in to pet her, but she swings her head out of reach. "I knew you'd love the hell out of her."

I smile, but feel sad for her at the same time. "I think it's too early to feed them all dinner."

"That's OK—we can go home and come back later," Micah says.

"Home?" I ask.

"Your house."

"Oh. Right." I love that Micah thinks of my home as his. Only I realize with a jolt that it won't be any of ours for long.

We help Ivy put Ferdinand back in his pen, then let the horses back out and find our bikes.

"Can we make an obstacle course again?" Ivy asks.

"Sure," I say. When we cross the street and go up the driveway, we see my dad's van. I imagine him inside with my mom. Maybe they're fighting. Or crying.

"I don't think we should go in," I say.

"Do you want me to go home?" Micah asks.

"No!" Ivy says. "We need you."

"You should stay," I say. "We can still make an obstacle course. We'll just keep away from Dad's van."

Micah and Ivy race to the garage to find some wood scraps and things to make ramps. I dig my shorts out of my backpack and put them on over my still-damp bathing suit. It feels gross, but it's better than walking around in just my suit, and better than risking going inside and seeing my parents. I sit on the front steps to wait. I don't hear any sound from behind the screen door. In fact the house seems almost too quiet.

I run my fingers over the fieldstone steps my dad repaired with stones he dug up in our woods. They aren't chiseled and perfect like the ones at the Townsends' house. I think they look nicer this way, and more natural. One time, a snake found its way to the lowest step and curled up in the sun. My mom came outside and stepped on it in her bare feet. The snake got scared and slithered through the open doorway. My mom went nuts and started screaming for me and Ivy. The snake slipped into the kitchen and got cornered near the refrigerator. "Don't take your eyes off it—I'll be right back!" my mom yelled.

She returned with the vacuum cleaner.

"What are you going to do?" Ivy cried. "Don't kill it! It's just an innocent old garter snake."

"I'm not going to kill it. I'm going to suck it up, and then we'll let it go outside."

Ivy looked doubtful, but I thought it was kind of genius.

"Rachel, plug me in," my mom said, moving closer to the snake with the vacuum tube.

I plugged her in, and the machine roared to life. My mom quickly aimed the hose at the snake, and it slipped right up the tube.

"Mom!" Ivy yelled. "I bet you hurt it!"

My mom kicked off her shoe and stuffed her sock in the end of the hose. "I didn't hurt it. Don't be silly. Now take this thing out to the woods and leave the vacuum bag out there so the snake can slither back out."

Ivy looked at me as if this was my job.

"You do it," I said.

"You'll both do it. Now."

Ivy carried the hose ahead of me while I lugged the body of the vacuum out behind the house and into the woods behind the barn. When we found a nice place near the big rock we loved to climb, Ivy slowly pulled out my mom's sock and I opened the machine to remove the vacuum bag. We put the two next to each other, then climbed onto the rock to watch from above and wait.

Ivy put the sock on her hand and pretended it was a puppet.

"Come on out, little snake," she made the sock puppet say. "You're safe and sound in the woods, where you belong."

We both peered down expectantly, but the vacuum bag didn't rustle and nothing slithered out of the hose.

"Mom killed it," Ivy said. She pulled off the sock and threw it at the bag. Just then, a little dark head poked out of the dusty bag and looked around.

"Shhh," I told Ivy so she wouldn't scare it back in.

Slowly the little snake inched out of the bag. It flicked its tongue at the sock before it wriggled under the old leaves on the ground and disappeared.

"See? She didn't kill it," I said. "It seems fine."

"Mom does weird stuff," Ivy said.

I jumped down off the rock and put the bag in the vacuum cleaner. "C'mon, help me bring this back to the house."

She followed behind me with the hose, moving the tube like a snake and hissing.

"Earth to Rachel!" Ivy says, sticking her face right in mine. Her breath smells like spoiled milk.

"When's the last time you brushed your teeth?" I ask.

She scrunches up her face in thought, then shrugs. "I don't actually remember."

"Gross."

She grins and blows her breath at me.

"Ack! You're killing me!"

She runs away and hops on her bike before I can grab her.

I watch her and Micah ride around, but my heart isn't in it. My heart is in these stone steps. It's in the big rock Ivy and I pretended was a cruise ship. A lookout tower. A safety zone in a sea of lava. My heart is in this driveway and all its cracks. It's in the wall with the school photos. It's in the paper lamp in my bedroom, and the curtains blowing in the breeze. It's in this house.

Home is where the heart is.

I can't imagine mine anywhere else.

❧ Chapter Twenty-One ❧

The screen door opens, and my mom and dad step out and sit on either side of me. My dad puts his arm around my shoulders, and I lean into him.

"I'm sorry, kiddo," he says quietly.

I reach my arms around his middle and hold tight. I want to cry but keep it in, knowing my tears will just make him feel worse.

My mom is quiet at my other side. I don't dare look at her. The three of us watch Ivy and Micah bike in circles, up and down ramps, swerving through marks they've made with chalk on the cracking pavement. Behind them, the old Bittersweet Farm sign seems to mock us. You can't have sweet without bitter.

"I should go take care of the animals," I say.

My mom doesn't respond, but my dad pats my back.

"You want company?"

I shake my head.

Ivy and Micah don't seem to notice me leave.

I go out back first to feed Rainbow and put him to bed in his stall. I try not to cry again, wondering where he'll go if we can't take him with us. "I love you," I tell him. "I love you so much." I press my face against his neck and hug him tight, then cross the street to the Townsends'. I feel like I'm walking out of bitter: old, worn house and beat-up driveway; to sweet: brand-new house with freshly paved driveway and new bushes planted just so.

I go through all the evening chores silently. The animals don't seem to notice.

I don't say hello when I carry Lucy's food to the fence and step up on the rung. As soon as she sees me, she jumps to her feet and trots over. She lifts her head and sniffs the air.

"Yes, I have your dinner," I tell her. "Same old same old."

She walks closer and stands by the fence.

"I'm not in the mood to be knocked over," I tell her.

She tilts her head slightly to one side.

"Got it?"

She waits.

I carefully lift the bucket over the top and set the handle in the hook.

Lucy keeps watching.

As soon as I step off the fence, she reaches her nose into the bucket and begins to eat slowly.

"Good girl," I say. She makes a contented sound as she snarfs down her food.

She finishes eating and walks in a circle, wiggling her tail. She reminds me of George when he's making a soft spot to lie down on.

"I don't know how much longer I'll be able to come visit you," I tell her. "We have to move."

She walks in another circle, then stops to watch me.

"If we don't move too far away, maybe I could still ride my bike here and come take care of you for the rest of the summer."

She tilts her head one way, then the other, as if she understands. Then she turns and goes under her shelter and plops down for a nap.

At the bottom of my driveway, I hear Ivy and Micah on their bikes. I walk slowly, carefully stepping over the familiar cracks in the pavement. The old house looks sad in the fading summer light. It needs a paint job, and some of the shutters hang at a tilt. My parents aren't on the steps anymore. I can see them through the kitchen window, putting something together for dinner. Probably spaghetti again.

"You left without telling us," Micah says, parking his bike in my way. "We would have come to help."

"You were having fun," I say. "And I kind of needed some time alone."

"Oh."

We both turn and look at the house together.

"I can't believe we won't be living here anymore," I say.

"I know."

Ivy continues biking in circles in the driveway. "Rachel! My cooling hole turned into a mudhole! Look!" She lifts up a muddy foot as she glides toward me on her bike. "I fell in and Micah had to pull me out!" She speeds up again and goes over a jump.

"Do you think she gets what's happening? She doesn't seem very sad anymore."

"Maybe she doesn't feel like she has that much to lose. She's younger than you. Different stuff makes her happy."

"I guess. Do you want to stay for dinner?"

"Nah, I should go home. Will you still go to Sierra's next party? Do you want to go together again?"

I shrug. "I don't know. I think it will be hard to be around all those happy people. And Sierra's fancy house. And . . . all the bikinis. I just don't fit in. Especially now."

"Maybe it would be good to be around friends who care about you."

"Who really cares about me besides you?"

"Lots of people, if you'd pay attention. What about Cybil? Besides, a lot of people have problems, Rachel. Maybe other people are going through tough times, too. I mean, maybe not the same as what's happening to you, but . . ."

"I know I'm not the only one with problems," I say, feeling irritated.

"Well, I'm just saying. Sometimes people are dealing with hard things at home. Or whatever. I don't mean to make you feel like what's happening isn't horrible. It is. I'm just saying—I don't know—everyone has a story. Don't assume everyone at that party is living the good life."

"OK," I say. He's really starting to annoy me, but I know he's right. "It's just that this house is more than just a house. It's more than just a home. It's . . . it's like I'm losing a member of the family. Every single good family memory I have happened here. Ivy and I were *born* here."

"I know," Micah says. "I'm sorry. Text me if you decide you want to go. I promise not to be a jerk."

"OK," I say. "Me too."

He pedals to the bottom of the driveway and stops. "Bye!" he calls.

Ivy yells back to him, but I just wave.

"Are you ready for some dinner?" I ask her.

"I'm always ready for dinner," Ivy says.

I help her brush off the dried mud from her legs and follow her inside to the kitchen. I was right about the spaghetti.

We all sit at the table when dinner's ready. My mom and dad look worn out. The only one who doesn't seem devastated is Ivy.

"So, where do you think we'll move to?" she asks. "Will we get a new house? Will we go to a new town so I can change schools? Can we move to a condominium? That's what my friend Harvey has, and it's great. His mom says she doesn't have to mow the lawn or shovel snow. You would like that, wouldn't you, Mom?"

My mom twirls spaghetti on her fork but doesn't bring it to her mouth. "Not now, Ivy," she says.

"But if we have to move, shouldn't we come up with a plan?"

"Ivy," my dad says, "there'll be time to figure it out later. Tonight's not the night."

"But I want to know what's happening," Ivy says. She's really wound up.

My mom keeps twirling her spaghetti, not saying anything.

"Don't be a jerk, Ivy," I say. "Can't you see Mom and Dad are upset?"

She shoves a huge forkful of spaghetti in her mouth, slurping the extra strands in, then chews with her mouth open.

"Gross!" I yell at her. "What is wrong with you?"

She opens her mouth wide to show her chewed-up food. A piece of spaghetti falls out of her mouth back onto her plate.

My dad slams his fist down on the table, and Ivy shuts her mouth fast.

My dad takes a deep breath to collect himself before he talks.

"Listen," he says, all serious. "Today has been a rough day for all of us."

My mom stares at her barely touched food.

"We don't know what's going to happen next. I know that sounds scary, but that's where we're at right now. Mom and I will go to the bank tomorrow and talk about our options and what we can afford. A lot of this depends on whether one of the school libraries your mom applied to for the fall reaches out. If not, she'll keep working part-time in the office with me, but money will be tight. We have to be patient. But whatever happens, we have each other. I know we all love this house, but it's just a house. We can make our home anywhere."

"Home is where the heart is," Ivy says, all cheerful. I want to punch her in the face. I've never wanted to hurt her like that before. But I don't want to go live in some strange place with no memories. That's not what home is.

"We can't just make any place feel like home," I say.

"Sure we can!" Ivy says. "It'll be an adventure!"

"No, we can't!" I yell. I sound like a baby, but I can't help it. I don't want to move. I don't want to go to a different school. I don't want anything to change.

Tears start to run down my mom's face.

"Well done, Rachel," my dad says, disgusted. "Now you've upset your mother again. I need you to act your age, if you don't mind."

"Maybe if you acted *your* age and were responsible with money, we wouldn't be in this mess," I blurt out.

My dad looks stunned and hurt.

"Rachel!" my mom yells. "Go to your room."

I glare at Ivy. "Gladly!"

I've never been sent to my room before. I've never gotten this angry before. Don't all the stories my parents have told us over the years about finding this house and making it special mean anything to them? Why didn't they try harder to stay?

"This is all your fault!" I yell at my mom. "You had to have this house you guys could never afford in the first place. But you made us all love it! You said you and Dad would grow old here and Ivy and I would visit when we had our own kids. And now we won't have anything! Home is *not* where the stupid heart is. Home is here and you ruined it!"

Ivy starts to blubber, and as shameful as it is, I'm glad.

I turn and stomp over to the couch, grab Ivy's stupid pillow, and rip the letters off it.

"No, Rachel!" Ivy cries.

I throw it on the floor as hard as I can and race up the stairs before they can yell at me for being so awful. I slam my bedroom door and pace back and forth, looking for something to throw again, or hit or kick or *something*. I know I'm acting like a spoiled brat. Not many kids in the world have their own bedroom, let alone live in a house. But right now it hurts anyway. Right now I don't want to think about all of that. I just want things to stay the same.

The cat jumps off my bed and runs to my door and meows to be let out. I quietly open the door and then shut it again. Even George doesn't want to have anything to do with me. I can't blame him, really.

I sit on my bed and take deep breaths, like Micah had me do earlier, but it doesn't help. I'm not anxious; I'm mad. Why couldn't my mom just get a different job when they cut her position at the library? Why couldn't my dad change jobs when real-estate sales got so hard and he stopped making enough commissions to get by? Why couldn't they do more instead of just waiting to run out of money and lose everything?

I walk slowly around my room, touching all the things that make it special. The bookcase my dad made for me, and all my favorite books. Some were my parents' when they were kids, like *Charlotte's Web* and *The Secret Garden* and *The Velveteen Rabbit*. And of course, *Paddington Bear*. I remember my mom and dad taking turns reading them to me, and then me reading most of them to Ivy, warning her when a sad or scary scene was coming. I wonder if there will be room for bookcases and books where we end up. Or if I'll be able to have my own room. There's so much I'll probably have to give away, like all the old toys I saved because they were too important to part with. I kneel down next to my old dollhouse and lift the roof to look inside. I haven't played with it in ages, but the little mouse family Micah and I made is still there. Mama Mouse is sleeping, and Papa Mouse is sitting on the couch. The brother is sitting at the kitchen table with the sister. And there's a baby in a tiny cradle in the bedroom. Micah and I used to spend hours playing with the mice. Sometimes we'd put them in my Fisher-Price school bus and pretend it was a camper and take it out to the sandpile behind the house, or the stone wall, and have them go camping. We'd make tents out of sticks and scraps of cloth, and once we made a mini campfire with a votive candle, but my mom found us and we got in trouble for playing with matches.

What will happen to the mouse family? My doll-house?

I put all the mice to bed and close the roof cover again.

This is all my parents' fault. I don't care if it's unfair to say or think—it's true.

I put my pajamas on, crawl into bed, and wait.

I don't know for what. Why would anyone come to check on me after that scene I made? I consider calling Micah, but I really don't feel like it. He'd just tell me I'm acting like a big baby and that I should go tell everyone I'm sorry.

Pretty soon, George scratches on the door to be let back in, but I ignore him. The breeze from outside is cool against my face. My old curtains dance out into the room like happy ghosts. I think of all the people who probably lived in this house before we did. The house is over two hundred years old, so that's a lot of people. Generations and generations. My mom always said the house wasn't haunted but that there was a friendly spirit here, watching over us. Sometimes strange things happen, like lights coming on in the middle of the night. And one time a glass fell off the hutch in the dining room for no reason. We knew there were explanations, but I think it was more exciting to make up stories about the friendly spirit. My mom called her Mrs. Harris because that was the name of the family who lived here before us. Someone told my mom that old Mrs. Harris, the grandmother, died in her sleep on a settee in the dining room. That's where the hutch is and that's where the wineglass fell. My mom said, "Mrs. Harris must be angry. What have you children done?" She was half joking, but Ivy took her seriously and refused to sleep in her own room for weeks. She set up a sleeping bag at the foot of my bed and insisted on sleeping there until I finally told my mom I needed my privacy and she made her go back to her room. I admit that once she was gone, I missed hearing her little snores, but not enough to invite her back.

What would Mrs. Harris do once we left? Would she come with us? Or stick around to keep the next family guessing? *I hope she haunts them,* I think selfishly. *I hope she scares them crazy.*

George scratches on my door again, and I finally get up to let him in. He rubs against my legs and follows me back to bed. He circles around my head, then settles against my neck and face. He purrs softly and starts to clean his paws. I rest my cheek against his side.

The soft vibration of his purring is like a lullaby that gently sings me to sleep.

ও Chapter Twenty-Two ৩

The house is quiet when I get up and go downstairs the next morning. I look for some carrots in the fridge but there aren't any so I head out back to feed Rainbow without any treats. I give him some grain, then bring him outside to graze for the day. I walk him around the yard first, talking quietly about our memories. Every so often, he sniffs my pocket to see if I have any treats. His nose is velvety soft, and when he breathes on me, it feels warm and comforting. I stop and hold the sides of his head in my hands so we can look at each other. His big brown eyes blink at me. His beautiful eyelashes have grayed a lot more since we adopted him, just like his muzzle. I press my forehead to his and breathe in.

He's quiet. Knowing.

"You are the best pony in the world," I tell him.

He jerks his head a little as if to agree.

I attach his lead to a longer rope, and he lowers his head to the dewy wet grass to graze. I reach down and braid his mane, humming to him as I do. I sing "Over the Rainbow" to him, then hug him again and bury my face in his warm coat. A big, heavy sob bubbles up out of me, then another. He lifts his head, confused. I hug him harder and sob into his neck.

"It's not fair," I say, crying harder.

He lifts one hoof and scratches it in the grass, oblivious that his life is about to change. Will another little girl get him for her birthday, like I did? Will she be kind to him? What if some jerks like the Grayson twins get him? What if they tease him and try to make him run and do tricks when he's too old and lazy for that? What if whoever adopts him doesn't give him treats, or braid his mane? Or read to him? Or tell him they love him?

My heart starts to beat faster, and I begin to feel the same panic I felt yesterday. Only this time, Micah isn't here to help me through it and I start to have trouble breathing. What if something bad happens to Rainbow? What if he isn't fed properly? What if he ends up all alone and neglected? I start to choke and gasp.

Then I feel pressure on my back.

"Rachel, calm down," my dad says.

I don't turn to look at him.

"Take a deep breath, honey. Slow down."

I try to slow my breathing, but I can't stop the uncontrollable sobs that roll out of me.

"Slowwwww breaths," my dad says again, more calmly. "In, then out."

I do as he says, and eventually the frantic feeling in my chest settles away.

My dad keeps rubbing my back in slow circles.

"I'm so sorry, honey. So, so sorry."

"What will happen to him, Dad?" I ask.

"I don't know. But I promise we'll find a good home for him. Hopefully someplace near us, so you can visit him whenever you want."

"What if he's sad? What if he isn't treated well? How can we make sure?"

My dad puts his hands on my shoulders and squeezes. He's quiet, which makes me more scared. It means he doesn't know how we can make sure. Maybe he knows we can't.

I turn around in his grasp to get a direct answer and discover that his face is streaked wet with tears. The only time I've ever seen my dad cry is the day Ivy was born, and those were happy tears.

"I'm sorry I was so mean to everyone last night," I say. "I'm sorry I ruined Ivy's pillow."

He pulls me to him so I can't see him cry. He must be even more scared than I am. And worried for all of us. I don't know how much our mortgage was, but if we can't afford to pay that, how will we pay rent somewhere?

"Dad?" I ask, the side of my face still pressed into him. "Are we going to be homeless?"

He squeezes me tighter. "No, honey. We'll figure something out. Mom and I have an appointment at the bank today. We'll know more after that. But we won't be homeless. We just . . . we'll have to live a lot differently."

"I'm scared," I say into his shirt.

He doesn't answer for a long time. Not even to say *We'll manage.* He just holds me. But it doesn't feel comforting. It doesn't make me feel like things will be OK or that I shouldn't feel scared.

I wait and wait for him to tell me not to be afraid, but he doesn't, which makes things feel even more scary. He's always been the one to make us believe everything is fine. That we'll get by. Or good news is just around the corner. This must mean that things are so bad, even he can't find a bit of hope.

"I'm afraid of what will happen to Rainbow and George," I finally say to break the silence.

"I know," he says quietly. "We'll do everything we can to keep George. Most places allow house cats. And I promise we'll try to find Rainbow the best possible home. He's easy to care for. And lots of people with horses like to have ponies to keep their horses company."

"But he'll think we abandoned him. He'll think we don't love him anymore."

My dad loosens his hold on me and runs his hand along Rainbow's back, over and over again. Rainbow doesn't seem to notice.

When you learn vocabulary words in school, you memorize the definition. And you have a good idea of what the words mean. But it's not until you feel them that you really grasp the definition. I've known what the world *helpless* means for a long time. And *desperate*. But I've never felt them. Feeling them is different. They fill your chest with a horrible sense of *dread* and *guilt* and *despair*. Those are more vocabulary words that you really can't fully understand until you feel them.

I feel them all now.

All together.

I feel them all, and I have never felt so awful in my life.

Ꮹ Chapter Twenty-Three Ꮜ

After I do chores across the street, Ivy and I spend the day watching *SpongeBob* episodes while we wait for our parents to get home from the bank. There's no sign of the ruined pillow, and I tell her how sorry I am for what I did. She gets quiet and shrugs, like she doesn't want to talk about it.

When our parents return, we run to the window to watch them and get a sense of how bad it is.

"They don't look too happy," Ivy says.

My mom pauses before she shuts the door of the van, as if she's trying to prepare herself for coming to tell us the news. My dad has a stack of papers in a folder under one arm.

"Should we pretend we're still watching TV?" I ask.

"I guess so." She slowly walks back to the couch. I think reality is setting in for her.

"Wait," I say. "This is dumb. Let's ask what happened. We need to know."

Ivy turns slowly and comes back to my side. We stand in the dining room and wait.

"Hey, guys," my dad says when he and my mom come in. He sets the papers on the messy table.

My mom stands a little behind him and seems to force herself to smile.

"Did they change their minds?" Ivy asks.

"No," my dad says.

"What's going to happen now?" I ask.

"Well—" He pauses and looks at my mom as if to get permission to tell us the truth.

She nods.

"We have to move. So the next step is to find a place. They gave us some options, and we have a plan."

"What kind of options?" I ask.

My mom is still being quiet, and I don't like the way it feels.

"There are some apartments near the high school that seem like a possibility. Your mom and I will probably go take a look tomorrow. We need to set up an appointment with the manager and fill out an application." He sounds like a robot.

"Can we go with you?" Ivy asks.

"Mmm, I don't think so. Let your mom and I go see what our options are, and then we'll go from there."

Ivy crosses her arms. "Well, there has to be space for George and Rainbow."

My dad takes a deep breath that looks like it hurts.

"Listen," he says. "About Rainbow."

"He's coming with us," Ivy says. "Right, Mom?"

My mom sucks in her bottom lip. That's what I do when I feel like I'm going to cry and my lip starts quivering.

"We have to!" Ivy says before my mom can say no.

I want to comfort her, but I don't know how.

"Apartment buildings don't have space for ponies," my dad says.

"But . . . what will happen to him?" Ivy is crying now. Big tears slip down her grimy cheeks and leave a cleanish trail. "We can't desert him!"

A tear slips down my mom's cheek, too. She quickly wipes it away. I don't think I've ever seen my family cry in my whole life as much as I have in the past two days.

"We'll find a good home for him," she says quietly.

"We will," my dad agrees.

Ivy looks at me. "You'll save him, won't you, Rach? Maybe Micah can keep him."

I hadn't thought of Micah before. "Maybe," I say. "We can ask."

"He'll do it," Ivy says. "I know he will. Micah loves Rainbow."

I put my arm over her shoulder and pull her to me. "We'll see," I say, which is what our parents always say when it's too hard to say no.

"It's not fair," she says quietly. "Poor Rainbow."

My dad turns to my mom. "I've got this," he says. "It's OK."

My mom turns and walks toward my parents' bedroom, probably because she doesn't want us to see her upset again.

"How about we go to the beach?" my dad asks. "Your mom and I took the day off because we weren't sure how long we'd be at the bank. It's not worth it to go to work this late in the day anyway. Let's not waste what's left."

"I don't want to leave," Ivy says.

"C'mon," I say. "I can't take another minute of *SpongeBob.*"

"I feel so sad," Ivy says, rubbing her tummy. "I feel like my body wants to be sick."

My dad and I exchange a look, and I feel helpless all over again. Between the three of us, we fill the room with this feeling.

"I want to go," I say. "I need to. You too, Ivy. Let's get out of here for a little while."

"Go get your suits on, and I'll meet you in the driveway," my dad says.

A few minutes later, I go out to the driveway to find my dad staring at the Bittersweet Farm sign. *OK,* I think, glaring at the sign. *There's been an awful lot of bitter around here. How about some sweet?*

"Hi," I say, stepping closer to my dad.

"Hi, honey." He sniffs and turns away from the sign. "You all ready?"

"Yup. Just waiting for Ivy."

We walk over to the van and get in. The faux-leather seats are hot and sticky. I put my towel under me to keep my skin from sticking to the plastic.

"We're going to be OK, Rach," my dad says. "I need you to know that. And I need you to know that your mom and I are sorry this happened."

"I know," I say. "You don't need to be sorry. You did your best."

He nods and starts the van when Ivy comes out and climbs in.

I'm surprised to see Micah at the beach when we arrive. A bunch of people from school are there, all hanging out at our end of the beach. I don't see any sign of Cybil, but I guess she's probably at work. I drop my towel down midway so we aren't near them.

"Why'd you stop here?" Ivy asks.

"I think we should have a family day," I say. "I don't really feel like seeing my friends right now."

She shrugs and drops her towel.

When Micah sees us, he sits up straighter on his towel and waves.

Ivy waves back wildly and motions for him to come over.

"I told you it was family day! Why'd you invite him over?"

"Micah is family," Ivy says.

"Fine."

My dad sits on his towel and looks out at the water.

"Hi, guys," Micah says when he reaches us.

I squint up at him.

"I would have invited you to come here today, but I thought you were avoiding people," he says.

"It doesn't matter," I say, a little more coolly than I meant.

"Want to go in?"

"Yes!" Ivy says, even though Micah was clearly asking me.

"I'm not hot enough yet," I say. "You guys go ahead."

Micah looks disappointed, but he turns and runs into the water, Ivy at his heels.

My dad and I sit next to each other on the edges of our towels and watch them.

"Is Mom going to be OK?" I ask. "She loves the house so much. It's like a family member to her."

I listen to my dad breathe for a while before he answers. He does this when he's trying to find the right words.

"Yes. She'll be all right. It's going to be really hard and sad at first, but we'll get through this. People go through much worse."

I think about the stupid "Could be worse!" family from that old book and feel a fist of anger tightening in my belly. It could be worse. It could be so much worse. I know it's true. But it still feels really, really bad.

"I wish we were rich, like the Townsends," I say.

My dad does his breathing thing again.

I'm sure he's going to give me some lecture about how money isn't everything, and I think of all the arguments I could give about how it sure doesn't hurt.

But instead, he sighs and says, "Yeah, that would be nice."

I lean into him, and he puts his arm around me.

"I love you, kiddo," he says. "And I'm really proud of you."

"I didn't do anything," I say.

"You've been a wonderful big sister this summer. And you've taken on a big responsibility with all those animals. You don't complain when your mom and I can't buy you things. You're just . . . you're a good kid, Rach. And you're teaching Ivy to be a good kid, too."

I think about all my inner griping about my bathing suit and hand-me-downs. Maybe on the outside I seem good, but I'm not always so great on the inside.

We sit like that for a while, watching Micah and Ivy play Clueless and float on their backs. They look like they're having a great time, but I don't really feel like joining them. Instead, I slather some sunblock on and lean back on my towel and let the sun warm my skin. I listen to the sounds of people playing in the water, and pieces of conversation of the people on towels nearby, and my dad's careful breathing, as if he's not just trying to come up with the right thing to say, but he's trying to figure out what on earth will happen to us. Where we'll go. And how we'll get by.

He breathes and breathes like that for a long time, but if he comes up with a solution, he doesn't share it out loud.

❧ Chapter Twenty-Four ❧

We spend the whole week and the weekend slowly packing things up. When I'm not doing chores at the Townsends', I'm home sorting through old clothes and toys or reading to Rainbow and Ivy. My mom gets a bunch of boxes from the local liquor store and tells Ivy and me that we have to be selective with our stuff and decide what we really want to keep. If there's something we haven't worn or played with for over a year, it goes in the Yard Sale box. If there's a special toy that we really want to keep even though we don't play with it, it goes in the For Discussion box. We show those things to her at the end of each day and then talk about why we want to keep them.

At first Ivy puts almost nothing in the Yard Sale box. She's always been kind of a pack rat. One Christmas, when she was five, she saved the wrapping paper from her three favorite presents and pinned it on her bedroom wall. We thought it was so cute. But when she puts the paper in her To Keep box, my mom tells her it's ridiculous.

Ivy starts to cry and tells her she needs the memories of that day. Then my mom starts to cry and gives in. But when she wants to keep some silly old duck towel that was mine when I was a baby and then hers, my mom puts her foot down. "We can't save everything!" she says, all annoyed.

By the third day, I join Ivy in her room and help her go through things to avoid end-of-the-day battles with my mom. I hadn't realized how many of my old toys she'd taken.

There are certain toys and books that, when I see them, bring me right back to the times when I played with them. I remember the stories I made up as I played with a certain doll or where I sat when I read certain books. I wish we could keep all this stuff and give it to our own kids, but there won't be room in our new place, wherever that will be, and we can't afford a storage unit. My parents seem to be on the phone all the time, talking with different housing people about available apartments. Every time they hang up the phone, they seem a bit more defeated, and it makes me scared that we aren't going to find a place to go. I spend less and less time talking with Micah, and I skip the party, too. All I want to do is sit in my room and hold the things I'm going to have to let go of.

And then I start getting messages from Cybil.

Missed you at the party.

Everything OK?

Can you come to the beach today?

Hope to see you soon.

I don't reply to any of them, even though a big part of me wants to. It would be fun to go to the beach and pretend nothing terrible was happening back at home. But I don't think I can do that right now.

Micah stopped by once to help me sort through things, but I can tell it depressed him just as much as it does me, so I told him he didn't need to.

Every day, the house disappears a little bit more as the packed boxes pile up. The bookcases are all empty. The pictures on the wall in the living room have been taken down, leaving bright squares on the walls where they used to be and the wallpaper hasn't faded.

When I feed Rainbow, I stay with him longer and longer, petting and brushing him and giving him extra carrots. My dad hasn't brought up the subject of where he might go, and I'm too scared to ask. I feel so guilty about it, I can hardly stand it.

I think George knows something sad is happening. He comes into my room and jumps in the boxes and meows, as if he wants me to stop packing everything away.

Finally, over the weekend, my dad gets off the phone and doesn't look defeated. "I think we've found a place," he says.

We all sit down at the dining-room table, which is covered with packing tape and markers and unopened mail.

My mom looks at him hopefully, but all I feel is dread. Somehow I hoped maybe there would still be a way to stay here.

"The apartments out by Route Twelve," he says.

My mom looks down at the messy table and squeezes her eyes shut, then opens them and forces herself to smile.

"Where's that?" Ivy asks.

"Near the highway," my dad says. "Way on the other side of town, where the school and library are."

Ivy thinks for a minute, and I can see her trying to picture the apartment building. It's tall and ugly and right next to the highway. It's surrounded by parking lots and the fast-food restaurants people stop at when they get off at the exit. It's the one I remember visiting for that birthday party when I was a kid. The one for people who can't afford to live anywhere else. I know this because we did a unit in social studies on homelessness and transitional housing and we learned all about the economics of our town and what kind of help there is for people when they lose their jobs and can't afford rent. We had a big discussion about how hard it is for people to get back on their feet when rents are so high and it's next to impossible to save money.

I can tell when Ivy realizes where the place is because her face sinks, and unlike my mom, she can't control herself when it comes to showing emotion. But she doesn't cry and she doesn't do anything babyish, like yell, "No! I won't go!" And that makes me sadder, really. Because it means she's lost hope.

"They have a two-bedroom available," my dad says. "We can go look this afternoon."

My mom nods, then gets up and walks over to an empty box and carries it into the living room.

My dad reaches across the table and touches my and Ivy's arms. "It's gonna be OK," he says. "It's temporary."

"What about Rainbow?" Ivy asks. "And George?"

"They allow cats but not ponies."

My heart sinks down into some dark part of me.

"We'll find him a good home — I promise."

I don't say anything because I hate it when people promise things they can't be sure of.

"Did you ask Micah yet?" Ivy asks me.

"No. You know he probably won't be able to take him. Where would they keep him?"

"They could make a stall in their garage!"

I sigh. I wish I could be that hopeful.

"Or maybe Sierra could take him. They have that big backyard."

"Their yard is a little fancy for a pony who will poop all over it," I say.

Ivy wipes her face with the back of her hand. "Well, at least I'm trying!" she yells. "If you really loved Rainbow, you'd be trying harder to find him a home!"

I think of all the ways I could respond to this. None of them are very nice and all of them would make my dad feel terrible, so instead, I get up and go outside to find Rainbow.

He's grazing on the lawn, swishing his tail, calm and unconcerned as always. I hug him and cry quietly into his dusty coat. I pet him and pet him and tell him what a good pony he is and how sorry I am that we can't keep him with us. He never pauses as he chomps on the grass. He just lets me cry into his back, swishing me with his tail, until I'm all cried out.

Maybe I should be glad he seems so indifferent. But really, it doesn't make things easier at all.

ᒰ Chapter Twenty-Five ᒡ

We spend another week packing like crazy. With each box packed, the house feels more empty. Over the weekend, we have the yard sale I've been dreading. My mom and dad have set up tables in a big U shape in the driveway and placed all the stuff we put in the Yard Sale boxes out on the tables for people to look over and take away. My parents didn't bother to put prices on anything because they couldn't agree on what to charge. Instead, people offer a few dollars for something and my parents take it. Sometimes Ivy pipes up and tells people something is worth way more than they've offered and my parents look horrified but try to laugh it off. They usually end up getting a tiny bit more and then Ivy looks all smug.

I hate it.

Sometimes people we know stop by. I can't tell if they're really interested in finding a deal, supporting my parents, or curious about what happened. It's uncomfortable. Every time I recognize someone, I pretend I need to get something in the house and wait inside until they leave.

It's so strange to watch people pick up our things, inspect them, and then either put them down again or take them away. It reminds me of visiting the thrift stores with my mom, and how each thing we got from those stores had a story, just like our things do. And now they've gone to some new home to add to their stories. Knowing that makes the whole ordeal feel a little less awful somehow.

By the afternoon, about half of our things are gone. My dad makes us sandwiches for lunch, and Ivy and I take ours out back and sit in the shade to eat near Rainbow. My mom made a sign that says FREE TO A GOOD HOME with a picture of him on it and put it in a frame on one of the tables, but so far no one has shown interest.

"What if we make so much money at the sale, we can pay off the house?" Ivy asks with her mouth full.

"We won't," I say. "We owe thousands of dollars probably, and we'll be lucky to make a few hundred today."

"That's because Mom and Dad are practically giving all our stuff away."

"That's because it's mostly junk."

She scrunches up her face and takes another bite.

"Rachel?" A familiar voice comes from the side of the house.

Ivy jumps up before I can and waves to Cybil as she comes around the corner.

"Hi!" she says, walking over to join us.

"Hi," I say. "What are you doing here?" I don't mean it to sound so unfriendly, but I can't seem to help myself these days.

"I heard you're moving," she said. "Did you get my texts?"

Ivy plops down next to me. "Want to have a picnic with us?"

"Sure." Cybil sits down on the old blanket we've brought out, and Ivy offers her a bite of her sandwich. "Uh, no thanks," she says. "I hope it's OK that I came by."

"Why wouldn't it be?" Ivy asks.

I roll my eyes. "It's fine," I say. "I'm sorry I haven't replied to you. I've been kind of busy."

"I understand." She glances over at Rainbow. "Cute pony."

"That's Rainbow," Ivy says. "We have to find a home for him."

"How come?"

"Because the apartment building we have to move to doesn't allow ponies," Ivy explains.

"You're moving to an apartment?"

"Yes, because we can't afford to live here anymore," Ivy says matter-of-factly.

"Oh."

"Ivy, maybe you could shut up," I say.

She takes another huge bite of her sandwich and glares at me.

"Sorry you have to move," Cybil says. "That stinks."

I shrug, feeling awkward.

"So, where is your apartment? Are you moving far away?"

"We're moving to the highway apartments," Ivy says through her mouthful of sandwich. "And Rachel and I get to share a bedroom! It's the only thing that makes moving not suck!"

"Ivy! Don't say that word!"

"Well, it's true. And learn how to take a compliment. Sheesh."

Cybil laughs. "The highway apartments?"

"By Route Twelve," I explain. "Where all the fast-food restaurants are."

"That's near the pharmacy!" Cybil says, perking up. "I was afraid you guys were moving far away. Maybe I can stop by after work sometimes and we could hang out. I mean, if you want to."

"Sure," I say absently. "That would be nice." It's just too hard to feel hopeful about moving, especially when we still don't know what's going to happen to Rainbow.

Cybil looks a little disappointed that I don't seem more excited.

"Sorry," I say. "I'm just having kind of a hard time."

"Oh, that's OK. I totally understand." She reaches over and squeezes my hand. "I hope it gets easier for you."

Her hand feels strong and firm on mine.

"Well, I should get going. I just wanted to stop by after I heard you were moving."

"Where did you hear it?"

She looks unsure about telling me. "Some people were talking about it at Sierra's party."

"Oh. Did they say why we were moving?"

Cybil scrunches up her face like she *really* doesn't want to talk to me about this.

"You can tell me," I say.

"People weren't really sure why, but one person

said her mom heard your parents had some financial problems. And then someone else said her parents heard the same thing. But people weren't really gossiping about you — I promise. They were just concerned. You know? And then Micah showed up and everyone stopped talking about it."

"Oh. Well, I guess it will be obvious when they find out where we have to move that we were having financial problems," I say.

Cybil shrugs. "It's not really anyone's business. Besides, plenty of people have money issues. It doesn't change who you are or anything."

Ivy has been sitting quietly on the edge of the blanket. "Money is overrated," she says.

Cybil laughs.

I roll my eyes. It's something my dad would say.

"I should go. I just wanted to make sure you were OK and to say good-bye, if you really were moving far away."

"Thanks," I say. We get up, and she gives me a quick hug. Ivy pops up and hugs her, too.

"She's nice," Ivy says, after Cybil disappears around the house.

"Yeah," I say. "She is."

By Sunday afternoon, most of the yard sale stuff is sold and I ask if I can go to Micah's house. He didn't come to the yard sale because he thought it would be too sad, and I agreed that having him here and seeing all the stuff we played with together disappear would be too hard. His mom left for a business trip and his dad is busy working in his office, so we go out to his yard to sit on the Adirondack chairs that circle a pretty firepit.

"Do you think you'll ever come back to the beach again?" Micah asks. He's wearing sunglasses that show my reflection in them.

"I don't know," I say. "I feel so awkward around everyone now."

"Why?"

"Because they feel sorry for me. Everyone knows why we have to move. Cybil told me they were all talking about it at the party."

"I didn't hear anyone talking about it."

"She said they stopped when you got there."

"Oh. Well, so what if they feel sorry for you? That just means they care about you."

"I guess."

"When did you talk to Cybil?" His eyebrows lift a little behind his sunglasses. I wish I could see his actual eyes because then I'd know if it hurts to act happy when he asks.

I shrug. "She came by the yard sale yesterday. She wanted to know if we were moving far away."

"Do you like her? Because she obviously likes you. A lot."

"How would you know?"

"Because she keeps asking when you're coming to the beach. And why you don't return her texts. And about a million other questions. Plus I saw you holding hands, so you must like her a little bit."

"That was only for like two seconds and I didn't know what to do. Besides, she was probably just being nice because she could tell I was sad about something."

"You mean, you didn't know what to do in the same way you didn't know what to do when Evan kissed you?"

I think about that. It *is* kind of like it in a way, but . . . not really. When Evan and I kissed, I felt disappointed and confused. When Cybil held my hand, I felt . . . comforted.

"I have a lot on my mind right now," I say.

Micah sighs. "Yeah, I know."

We're quiet for a little while. I realize I don't know much about Cybil at all. I have no idea where she lives

or what kinds of things she likes to do for fun, besides
go to the beach. And I don't know if . . .

"So do you like Cybil or not?" Micah asks, as if reading my mind. "And don't say you don't know."

"But—"

"C'mon, Rach. Just tell me."

"It's personal," I say. "If I like Cybil, that's my
thing. I know this is your way of helping me 'come
out' or whatever, but I'm not ready to do that. At least
not officially. I just want to get used to feeling how I
feel. I don't want a label on me. Not yet. But when
I know for sure, I'll tell you. I promise. Right now, I
just need to . . . I don't know. Not worry about it so
much."

He nods quietly. I really don't like those glasses.

"What about you?" I ask. "Any progress with Sierra?"

"You know I don't like her."

"Sam?"

"Nah."

"Anyone?"

He shrugs. "When I know for sure, I'll tell you," he
says. But not in a mocking way.

"Are you OK?" I ask. "I know this must be hard for
you, too."

"Yeah, I'll be all right. At least you guys aren't

moving to another town. And it's not that bad of a bike ride, right?"

"Right."

We're quiet again. I think we both know things are about to change in all kinds of ways, not just because I'm moving. It feels scary, and sad.

"Micah?" I ask. I reach over and take his sunglasses off so I can see his eyes. "Whatever happens, you will always be my best friend and I will always love you."

He smiles at me and his eyes get a little glassy, like he might cry. But he doesn't.

"I should go home," I say. "Hopefully the sale is over by now."

"Want me to bike back with you?"

"Nah, that's OK. See you tomorrow?"

He nods and I stand up to start toward the driveway where my bike is.

"Hey, Rach?" Micah calls.

I turn. "Yeah?"

"I love you, too. Best friends forever."

It's the first time he's used that term. No more *together forever*. But *best friends*.

He's wearing his sunglasses again, so I can't see his eyes. I give him my dorkiest double thumbs-up and walk away.

ᓚ Chapter Twenty-Six ᓯ

After dinner on Sunday night, Mr. Townsend shows up carrying a small cooler. He also has my check for the week. When my mom invites him in, he sets the cooler on the floor and seems at a loss for words. All of us are.

"Mrs. Stearn from down the street told me what happened with the house," he says. "I . . . I'm so sorry. What a shame. I wish there were something I could do."

"I can still take care of the animals for the rest of the summer," I tell him. "I can ride my bike over."

"Oh, oh, good. I hadn't even thought of that."

We all look at one another awkwardly, until Ivy blurts out, "I know how you can help! You could take Rainbow! He would love it at your place."

My mom makes a horrified face.

"Rainbow?" Mr. Townsend asks.

"Rachel's pony! We can't keep him because we have to move to an apartment building that will only let us take George."

"George?"

"Our cat. Rainbow is real easy to take care of. He's small, so he doesn't eat a lot, and he never bites or kicks. He likes to be brushed, and he loves carrots."

I know that what Ivy has done is totally inappropriate, but I'm also grateful, because Mr. Townsend actually looks like he's considering it.

"We only have the two horse stalls," he begins.

"Oh, Rainbow can sleep anywhere!" Ivy says. "He doesn't need a fancy stall, does he, Rachel?"

"No," I say. "He isn't picky at all. He could even stay in the stall you use as a tack room."

"Hmm. Maybe we could divide it up, if he's as small as you say. Well, I'll have to discuss it with Greer. . . ."

Ivy looks like she's about to explode with excitement. "You should come meet him! Right now! Once you meet him, I just know you'll love him!"

My parents both seem mortified. Usually they would try to shut Ivy up, or apologize. But instead they just stand there looking helpless.

"OK, OK," Mr. Townsend says. "But first let me give this to your parents." He puts the cooler on the dining-room table. "Some pork for you," he says. "Greer and I couldn't possibly eat it all ourselves. We'll have some bacon to share, too."

"Oh," my mom says, looking confused.

But I realize now what's in the cooler.

"Sorry, Rachel," he says to me. "I know you were getting attached. But she wasn't much longer for this world anyway, and the vet thought the sooner the better, so . . ."

He's still talking, but I'm not listening.

I stare at the cooler.

He keeps looking at me apologetically.

Ivy hasn't clued in yet. She grabs my hand and says, "C'mon, Rachel! Let's introduce Mr. Townsend to Rainbow!" but I shake her off somehow.

My mom waves her away, and I think I hear her say, "Go on—we'll be out in a minute." But I'm not sure because I'm staring at the cooler and I know what's happened and my worn-out heart is racing again and I think this time it is going to break.

My dad grabs the cooler and goes into the kitchen, and Ivy and Mr. Townsend follow behind.

"Rachel?" my mom says. Her hands reach my shoulders, and she moves her face in front of mine. "Are you OK?"

I close my eyes so I don't have to look at her.

"Rach?"

The back door slams.

I take deep breaths like Micah taught me. I hold them in and count to five before I let them out.

"They killed Lucy," I finally say. "I've been taking care of her all summer. They didn't even warn me! They didn't even let me say good-bye! I thought I'd have a chance to save her! I should have tried sooner, but I got so caught up in the house and—"

"Rachel, calm down or he'll hear you," my mom says.

"They killed her!"

"Rachel, stop."

She leads me into her and Dad's bedroom and shuts the door. I sit on the edge of their bed and heave up sobs from deep in my belly. My mom closes the bedroom windows and then comes to sit beside me.

"Rachel, it's a farm. You know this is how things work on farms."

"I was sure they'd change their minds about her. They seem so nice. And Lucy was finally starting to trust me."

My mom sighs and rubs my back.

"We were friends!"

"Oh, Rachel," my mom says. "I'm sorry."

"He could have at least told me when they were going to do it so I could say good-bye!"

"Maybe he didn't realize how attached you'd become. He seems like a nice man. I'm sure if he'd known, he wouldn't have handled it this way."

"Please don't put her in our freezer, Mom. Please don't. I can't stand the thought of it."

"No, honey, we won't."

"Why is everything so unfair? Why can't one good thing happen?"

My mom squeezes me closer. "I don't know, honey. But—"

"Don't say it could be worse. Just don't."

"But—"

"Just don't. I know it could. But just don't."

We sit on the bed quietly, my mom rubbing my back. Around the room, open boxes litter the floor. Some are overflowing, some half-filled. It looks like my mom is having just as much trouble parting with things as Ivy and I are. She still hasn't taken our baby photos off the wall.

My mom notices me staring at them. "I couldn't bear to see blank squares on the wall," she says. "I'll save taking those down for last."

A door slams and then excited footsteps run through the house. "Rachel! Rachel!" Ivy shouts.

"In here!" my mom calls.

She opens the door, her face glowing. Then she sees my teary one and droops.

"What's wrong?" she asks.

I realize she still hasn't figured out that the pork in the cooler is Lucy. And that Lucy is dead. And I don't have the heart to tell her.

I wipe my face. "Nothing," I say. "What's up?"

"Mr. Townsend is going to take Rainbow! He loves him and said he knows Mrs. Townsend will, too! And Rainbow licked his hand and you know he only ever does that to you! So that means it's meant to be!"

Her T-shirt is filthy as usual. I bet her hair hasn't been washed in ages. She looks a little nuts. But she also looks happy. I haven't seen her look like that since I let her beat me at Monopoly.

I never thought I'd be glad to be sending Rainbow away, but I realize there couldn't possibly be a better place for him to go. And he'll have so much company—and wooden floors, just like Micah and I wished for back at the beginning of summer.

My dad appears in the open doorway. He looks happy, too. Relieved.

"Did you hear the great news?" he asks.

I nod.

My dad sees that I've been crying, but I'm glad he doesn't ask why. I know my mom will take care of things.

"Let's go do some packing," I say to Ivy.

She follows me upstairs and runs to her room. In my own room, I lie down on my bed and look out the window at the Townsends' house next door. I picture Rainbow there, getting special treats from the mini fridge and spending the nights with gentle Ben and Gil. It's a better home than here. It's a better life than we could ever give him.

But then I think of Lucy and her empty pen. I know it's part of farm life, what Mr. Townsend did, but it still feels awful. *I* feel awful. Awful, and all mixed up.

Awful and *sad*.

More words I don't think I've ever felt so deeply. I would really like to feel a positive word for a change.

ꗈ Chapter Twenty-Seven ꗈ

Yesterday morning, after Ivy said good-bye, I brought Rainbow to his new home and did the morning chores. He took to Ben and Gil right away. I introduced him to all the animals, carefully avoiding Lucy's area, and by the time I left him, he was right at home. He didn't even seem to notice it was good-bye when I hugged him — he was so busy sniffing all the new smells and checking out all his new friends. He's happy here, I told myself. And that made me happy, too, even though I was also sad. This is what *bittersweet* feels like, I thought as I walked away. But it felt more sweet for once.

Today is moving day, so I asked Mr. Townsend for the day off because there's so much work to do. Micah and his dad come to help us pile all the furniture and

boxes into a big moving truck. The house slowly emp-
ties out until there's nothing left. As I walk through
each room for the last time, my footsteps echo in the
emptiness, reminding me that we really are leaving for
good. It doesn't even feel like our house anymore, all
empty and sad looking, which makes it just a tiny bit
easier to say good-bye.

Micah, Ivy, and I get in the van with my mom and
follow behind the big moving truck. We drive through
town to our apartment building. It's called Applewood
Heights, which sounds like a map section in a fairy-tale
book but looks nothing like one. There are no apple
trees in sight and definitely no woods. Maybe they cut
down all the trees to make the apartment building,
which would just figure.

People look out their apartment windows as we
start to unload. We each take a box and follow my dad
inside, where he picks up a key from the office on the
first floor. We stack the boxes in an elevator and squeeze
in. We quietly watch the red digital numbers rise: 1, 2,
3, 4, then *ding*. When my dad unlocks the door to the
apartment, it does not feel like stepping over some special threshold to our new home, like they show in movies. It smells funny inside, and the carpeting looks old
and worn. You can see matted-down trails in the rug

where the people who lived here before us walked from the kitchen to where their couch must have been, and then to the hall that leads to the bedrooms.

My dad tries to look enthusiastic but can't manage it. We put the boxes in their designated rooms and then head back down for more. It takes all day. The furniture is the worst because some of it won't fit in the elevator and we have to drag it up the fire-escape stairs. Some of the residents come out and help, as if it's their way of welcoming us to the neighborhood. They seem friendly and nice, and already this place is feeling less gloomy than it did when we first stepped inside.

By the end of the day, we're all dripping in sweat, and my dad suggests we leave things and go for a swim, but none of us can remember which boxes our bathing suits are in. Instead, Mr. Sasaki gets us pizza and we sit at our kitchen table, which looks so out of place in the tiny kitchen eating area here and not in our house on the hill. I think he can tell we all feel awful, because he eats really fast and tells Micah they should give us some peace and time to rest. They offer to come over tomorrow to help unpack, but my mom tells them we can manage and thank you and she sort of pushes them out the door even though they're clearly ready to go anyway.

When she closes the door, she leans against it and looks from left to right, at the strange cabinets in the kitchen that aren't wood but some kind of white particle board, and the ugly light-blue laminate countertops, and the scratched linoleum floors with a flower pattern. Her shoulders start to shake, but she takes a deep breath and doesn't let herself cry.

"Let's go make our beds," I say to Ivy.

In our room, which is smaller than the rooms either of us had at home, I try to put on a good face and rearrange the cardboard boxes until I find the one that says BED LINENS. We open the box, and we make our beds, which barely fit foot to foot along the wall. I tell Ivy that opening the boxes is kind of like opening presents at Christmas, but she makes a face and says, "That is the dumbest lie you've ever tried to feed me."

I am so surprised by this that I start to laugh and I jump on the empty linens box and squash it. Ivy helps me. We flatten that thing like a pancake.

"That felt good!" she says. So we unpack some more and slowly empty boxes and then demolish them.

After a while, my dad comes in to check our progress and take the empty boxes down to the big recycling container outside.

Even when I hang up the paper lantern I made with

Micah, this room does not feel like home. It does not feel like it ever will. I try to remember my dad's promise, that this is only temporary. And maybe it will be. But for now it mostly feels like sorrow.

The next morning, my dad asks me if I want to come with him to the house for a final walk-through to make sure we didn't leave anything, and to pick the vegetables from the garden. Since I need to do chores at the Townsends', this saves me one bike ride, so I agree, even though I don't want to go back and see our sad empty house again.

When we pull into the driveway, I can tell this is going to be even harder than I thought. My dad gets out first and stands under the Bittersweet Farm sign. Then he unties the ladder from the roof of his van and brings it over. I watch from below as he carefully pries the sign from the garage.

"Help me, will you?" he asks.

I reach up for one end of the sign and hold it above my head while he moves the ladder over to the other end of the sign and loosens it, then lowers it. We carry it over to the van and tie it onto the roof. I don't ask him what he plans to do with it. And I don't tell him it feels a little wrong to take it. There's a long strip of fresh-looking red paint where the sign used to be, and it makes the rest of the garage look even more worn out than it did before.

"I've got some things to collect in the garage," he tells me. "Why don't you head across the street and get your chores done, and I'll meet you in the garden."

"OK," I say. The house doesn't feel right, all empty inside, and I'm grateful not to have to go back in.

Across the street and behind the Townsends' fancy new house, I see Rainbow waiting in the corral with Ben and Gil. He whinnies happily when he sees me, like, "Look at me in my new amazing home! Look how lucky I am!" It makes me feel happy and sad at the same time. Bitter and sweet all over again.

As I go through my morning routine, I almost start to make Lucy's feed before I remember she's gone. I hate walking past her pen and seeing it empty. The weeds are already starting to grow in her mud spot.

After I gather eggs and take Ferdinand for his walk, I give Rainbow some extra love. He really does seem happier over here, and it makes me feel bad that maybe he didn't have the best life with us. Maybe we weren't a good family for him after all. It's strange that before he came here, I thought his life was over. Maybe if losing our house isn't the end of the world for Rainbow, it won't be for us, either. But when I think of my dad pulling down that sign, and the way my mom always seems to be trying to swallow down her tears, I just don't know.

"Hey, Rach!" my dad calls, coming down the path. "Do you need some help? I was about to give up on you."

"Sorry, it takes a while to get everything done."

He nods and pats Rainbow. "Hey, buddy. You look happy."

Rainbow sniffs his hand for a treat.

"Nice place here, huh?" my dad says, looking around.

"Yeah," I say. Before, I would have given him a tour and introduced him to everyone, but I can tell he's anxious to go.

I follow him back over to our side of the street and out to the garden. He's piled a bunch of paper bags at the garden gate and gestures for me to take one.

"Pull everything up," he tells me. "Even if it's not ripe."

I look at him funny, as if to ask, "Why bother?" but he's already busy at one end of the carrot row, pulling up these pathetic skinny carrots that are nowhere near ready to eat.

"Dad," I start, but he pulls with more eagerness and I know now is not the time to argue.

I make my way over to the hard green tomatoes and twist them off their vines, placing them carefully in the used paper bag. I'm so busy prying the tomatoes, I don't realize my dad has stopped until I finish and make my way to the zucchini. His back is to me, and he's kneeling in the dirt, his hands covered in dark soil. I would almost think he's praying by how still he is. As if he's trying to stop time.

Quietly I make my way to the zucchini and pick every last little one. The leaves sting my hands as I lift them to look under and make sure I got everything. Then I move on to the cucumbers. I work around my dad and pull up everything from the garden, filling all the bags with vegetables we'll probably never eat. The only thing that seems edible so far is the lettuce. I pull up the heads from their roots rather than pinch the leaves off like my mom does to keep them growing. Then the basil plants. And the cilantro. All of it. When I'm finished, the garden looks like it does when it's ready to be planted at the start of summer. Loose soil in long, neat rows set and turned by my dad.

I bring all the bags to the van. It takes several trips,

and each time, I pause and check on my dad. His back rises and falls slowly, but he doesn't get up. Finally I finish and walk over to him. I put my hand on his shoulder in a gentle way, then kneel beside him. He brushes his face with the back of his hands and smears dirt across his forehead. We don't talk, kneeling in the cool soil. Just sit in our garden and try to remember it as best we can. I hope someday soon we'll have another home like this. Someday soon, we'll be able to move out of that unfamiliar apartment and have a new old place to fix up and make memories in.

Eventually my dad gets up and holds out a soil-covered hand. I take it and he pulls me to my feet, and then into a long hug. I'm glad my dad and I don't need words to say how we're feeling.

"Do you want to go in for one last good-bye?" he asks me back at the van.

We both stare up at the old house.

"I don't think so," I tell him. "I don't think I want to go in there now that everything that made it home is gone."

"OK, honey. I understand." He pats my back.

I picture the messages Ivy and I wrote inside our closet doors, and what the people who move in will make of them. Ivy wrote, *Ivy lived here. Please take care of this room. And don't be afraid of Mrs. Potter.* I wrote my name, the dates we lived here, and *This is a special house.*

I realize now that Ivy's silly pillow is right. Without us, without all the things that make us a family, this place really is just a house. I think there will always be traces of our hearts here, like our sad notes inside our closet doors, but home is what the four of us are together, wherever we go.

"Ready?" my dad asks quietly.

"Ready," I say. We climb into the van and slowly roll out of the driveway for the last time.

❦ Chapter Twenty-Eight ❧

Back at the apartment, my dad and I take several trips to bring up all the vegetable bags. My mom and Ivy have managed to unpack a lot more boxes, and the apartment is starting to feel less empty and a little more homey.

When my mom peeks in one of the bags and sees the carrots, she sighs but doesn't say anything.

Ivy grabs one and cleans it in the sink, then takes a bite. "Is this how they make baby carrots?" she asks.

I roll my eyes.

"Rachel, be nice," my mom says.

My dad tousles Ivy's hair, then reaches for a black trash bag I saw him carry up. I don't remember putting anything in a plastic bag.

My mom opens it and pulls out several bittersweet vines my dad must have cut for her while I was at the Townsends'. My mom puts her hand to her mouth.

"Don't cry," my dad says. "These are to cheer you up. I thought Ivy could help you make a wreath."

Ivy comes bounding over to grab them from my mom.

"Careful, you'll knock the berries off before they can even open," my mom says.

Ivy calms down and touches the vine. "I want to make it myself," she says.

"All right." My mom helps her pull the rest of the vines from the bag and lay them out on the counter.

My dad and I leave them and go back to the van.

We untie the Bittersweet Farm sign from the roof and carry it up the four flights of stairs. It's hard to navigate through the narrow stairwell, and then through the door of the apartment.

My mom's mouth drops when she sees what we have. At first I think she is about to start yelling at my dad. Or crying. But instead she starts to laugh.

"What on earth do you think we're going to do with that old thing?" my mom asks.

George pops out of an open box and mews, then comes over to circle my legs.

"I don't think George counts as a farm animal," I say.

"Well, you've certainly brought home the entire garden!" my mom says.

My dad directs me to walk into the living room, where the old couch is set up against the wall that faces two windows looking out over the parking lot and highway beyond.

My dad sets some drywall screws into the wall, and then together we lift up the sign and hang it in place.

Ivy and my mom watch and direct us so we hang it straight. When we finish, we step back. It looks terrible. The sign is dirty and needs a paint job. Against the newly painted white apartment wall, it seems even worse. Still, somehow, it fits.

"To remind us that we'll have another Bittersweet Farm to hang this at someday—I promise," my dad says.

I really don't like these kinds of promises, but maybe if his promise for Rainbow worked out, this one will, too.

George hops back into a box and scratches at the cardboard. Ivy kneels down and scratches the outside of the box and mews at him. He goes nuts and jumps out to see what's on the other side, making Ivy giggle.

My dad gets busy in the kitchen, cleaning and organizing the vegetables. My mom unpacks more boxes.

I walk to the tiny bedroom I share with Ivy now and stand in the doorway. Her bed is neatly made and on top of her regular pillow is the old *Home Is Where the Heart Is* pillow. She's stitched the letters back on and sewed the stuffing back inside. I pick up the pillow and sit on my own bed, tracing the letters with my finger the way Ivy does to comfort herself. Then I pull out my phone, which I've been avoiding for days. There's a long scroll of old texts from Micah, inviting me to come to the beach soon. I text him to say thank you for helping with the move.

Thanks for being my best friend, I write. *See you soon!*

Just as I finish, a new text pops up. It's from Cybil.

Thinking of you. How was the move? Want to meet up?

There's a strange feeling in my chest — something I haven't felt in so long, I forgot it was possible. My heart feels like a hummingbird waking up and starting to flit excitedly. Happily.

I take one of Micah's deep breaths and count to five, then let it out. But my heart still flutters in my chest, urging me to smile. Urging me to let myself feel good again.

I take another deep breath and hold it, smile, and let it out.

Hey, I write back. *I'd love to.*

Acknowledgments

I owe thanks to many people for supporting me in the creation of this book. First, to my editor, Joan Powers, who encouraged me to pursue the project in the first place and gently guided me through many drafts. Also to my agent, Barry Goldblatt, for cheering this project on. As always, to my writing partners and dear friends, Debbi Michiko Florence and Cindy Faughnan, for their valuable feedback. Thank you to my husband and first reader, Peter Carini, and my mom and dad, Judi and Malcolm Knowles, who taught me where home is. Thanks also to my son, Eli Carini, for the many long talks about the conflict and plot — your encouragement meant everything, Eli. Speaking of encouragement, thanks to Craig Childs for the many discussions that planted the seeds for this story and the helpful writing prompt that got me started. Finally, a giant thank-you to my publicist Jamie Tan, second reader Allison Cole, and everyone at Team Candlewick Press for their continued support. You all make my heart beat like a hummingbird with joy and deep gratitude.

Discussion Questions

1. The title of this novel is drawn from the common expression "Home is where the heart is." How is Rachel's heart changed when her family is forced to leave Bittersweet Farm?

2. "This is all my parents' fault," Rachel decides when she learns that her family is losing Bittersweet Farm (page 239). "I don't care if it's unfair to say or think—it's true." Do you agree? Who—or what—else could be to blame?

3. In Rachel's town, there are some very rich families living alongside some very poor ones. What are some of the obvious signs of wealth in Rachel's community? What are the telltale indicators of financial strain?

4. Every vote always matters, but in small-town elections a single vote can have immediate and obvious consequences. Why is it so hard for the Gartner family to recover from the loss of Mrs. Gartner's job after the town votes down the school budget?

5. How well do Rachel and her parents communicate with each other? How honest are they with each other? How do they look after each other's needs?

6. How would you rate Rachel as a big sister? What responsibility do you think older siblings should have for younger children in the family? What do younger children owe their older siblings?

7. "Do you miss being a kid?" Ivy asks her older sister (page 125). "Yeah," Rachel replies. "All the time." How would you answer Ivy's question?

8. As young children, Rachel and Micah vowed to marry each other, but now she feels differently. "I'm filled with guilt," she says (page 3). Why does she feel guilty? What does she mean when she later says "I love him, but I don't *love* him" (pages 64–65)? Why is Rachel jealous when she sees Micah with other girls?

9. "I just want to get used to feeling how I feel," Rachel insists (page 270). "I don't want a label on me." Yet other kids in her class are happy to be labeled as gay or straight. What are the disadvantages of having a label? What are the advantages?

10. The health class teacher assures her students that they can safely explore sexual identity in her class, but Rachel has her doubts: "I don't know if in the real world people are all that open-minded" (page 136). Do you share Rachel's concerns? How open-minded is your school community about sexual identity? How open-minded is your larger community?

11. There are no talking spiders on Rachel's farm, but references to *Charlotte's Web* are found throughout the book. How does E. B. White's classic compare to *Where the Heart Is*?

12. "It's gonna be OK," Rachel's father says about their new apartment (page 259). "It's temporary." Try to imagine what the future holds for Rachel's family. Are you as confident as Mr. Gartner that the family will be OK? Why?

TWO MORE SENSITIVE, POIGNANT,
AND SWEETLY FUNNY NOVELS FROM JO KNOWLES

"A clear-eyed, gently humorous novel." —*The Washington Post*

Available in hardcover and paperback and as an e-book

"Heartbreaking, soul-sustaining, and all-around beautiful." —Rebecca Stead, author of the Newbery Medal winner *When You Reach Me*

Available in hardcover, paperback, and audio and as an e-book